Lonely and confused, Jenna McLean finds it difficult to plan for her future.

Why was it that some people were so sure of what God wanted them to do? Stacie had been so sure that God had wanted her to work at a new homeless shelter that she had almost lost Brad. Even Brad had been surprised that Stacie would let him break their engagement because he did not want her to move away for a new job. In the end, everything had worked out, but Jenna had never forgotten what Stacie had been willing to do because she had been convinced of what God had wanted her to do.

Dillon had been just as sure that he was supposed to leave the homeless shelter to run the camp, and he had thrown himself into the task without looking back for even a moment. Fighting incredible odds, he had pulled the sinking camp from the snatches of financial ruin. Now, there was every reason to think the place would succeed.

For Jenna, God's Will always seemed like a murky, choking river that she was not sure she could cross.

SUSANNAH HAYDEN is the pen name of a versatile and gifted author of fiction and biography for both adults and children. Susannah makes her home in Illinois with her husband and children.

Books by Susannah Hayden

HEARTSONG PRESENTS
HP14—A Matter of Choice
HP69—Between Love and Loyalty
HP77—The Road Before Me

ROMANCE READER—TWO BOOKS IN ONE
RR9—Summer's Wind Blowing & Spring Waters Rushing

Between the Memory and the Moment

Susannah Hayden

A sequel to *Between Love and Loyalty*

Heartsong Presents

A note from the Author:

I love to hear from my readers! You may write to me at the following address:

Susannah Hayden
Author Relations
P.O. Box 719
Uhrichsville, OH 44683

ISBN 1-55748-671-9

BETWEEN THE MEMORY AND THE MOMENT

one

"What is all that commotion?" Jenna McLean literally popped up off the love seat in her cozy living room and pushed aside the curtain on the picture window. Her stone cottage, situated just inside the entrance to the old Family Homestead camp, served as a watchtower for everyone coming and going through the wide gates. Jenna's blue eyes squinted against the glare of the sun outside; her long wispy blond hair curled at her temples in the early summer humidity.

Outside, a familiar delivery truck, its bright yellow logo emblazoned on a muddy brown background, backed up and screeched to a halt at one end of the drive that arched in front of Jenna's sturdy cottage.

Stacie Davis joined the inspection at the window. Together they watched three young men gesturing and maneuvering around the parking lot. Dillon Graves, the one in charge, pointed up the hill where the lumber should be stacked.

"Must be a guy thing," Stacie said. "Seems like when Brad and Dillon get together out here they get crazy."

Jenna dropped the curtain back in place. "That delivery guy doesn't help."

"You mean Doug? I thought you liked him."

"I do. He's very reliable and has a good sense of humor. But every time he comes out here with something, he has to cut the corner just a little closer or rev the engine just a little louder. I'm convinced he just likes to aggravate Dillon."

"Where did Dillon find him anyway?" Stacie asked,

settling back into the rocking chair.

"He works for a lumberyard Dillon orders a lot of stuff from. He didn't used to come out here much, but it seems like he does all the deliveries to the camp now."

Stacie tucked a plaid throw pillow behind her back for support. "Probably no one else wants to drive this far out of town just to drop off a few boards."

"Well, despite all his shenanigans, Doug seems nice enough. I've talked to him a few times."

Jenna looked over at Stacie, seven months pregnant and her ankles swollen to twice their normal size. "Are you comfortable, Stace?" Jenna asked. She bent at her conspicuously thin waist and pushed an ottoman toward Stacie. "Here, prop your feet up."

Stacie looked genuinely grateful for the footrest. "I may never be able to get up now."

"I'm not very experienced at this pregnancy stuff," Jenna said, dropping back into the forest green love seat she had bought only a few weeks ago, "but it's hard for me to imagine that you still have six weeks to go."

Stacie nodded in agreement. "I haven't seen my feet for weeks. I'm way past the excited-to-be-pregnant phase."

"How do you manage to get up and go to work every day?"

Stacie shrugged. "Mostly habit, I guess. And I like my work so much. When Dillon quit working at the shelter so that he could run this camp, I never imagined I'd get to be the director."

"Dillon says you're doing a great job."

A look of slight embarrassment crossed Stacie's face. "Well, I'm doing my best. But I'm not superwoman. I want to work part time for a couple of years after the baby is born."

Jenna looked up, surprised. "Oh? Dillon never mentioned that."

"I told him only a couple of days ago, just in case he wanted to come back."

"Does he?"

"No. He loves it out here. He says he's doing his part by creating a camp that some of the homeless families can come out to on weekends."

"Then who will run the shelter?"

Stacie shrugged again and ran a tired hand through her cropped copper-colored hair. She had worn it long for years but, with a job and the baby on the way, she had finally given in and gotten a more practical cut. "That's the problem. There really isn't anyone right now. . ."

"And you're running out of time," Jenna completed the thought. From their seats the two young women gazed out the window. Jenna remembered the first time she had come out to the old Family Homestead. It was hard to believe it had been three years since the young adult group at the church had worked to renovate the camp and get it running again after years of idleness. She had been a sophomore at the local college and joined the project because she thought most of the men in the group would be working.

Silently, Jenna shook her head at her own youth and foolishness. What a wretched motive for being involved in such a worthy project.

Fortunately good things had come of it. She had gotten to know Mrs. Margaret Barrows, the original owner of the camp, and was able to help care for her in the months before her death. Then she had gotten to know Dillon Graves, the new owner, who let her continue to live on the grounds in the comfortable old stone cottage that Mrs. Barrows had occupied. Dillon himself lived in a remote cabin, with no telephone, on the other side of the hill, but he seemed content. And the project had led to some genuine friendships with other people in the church group, for which Jenna was grateful.

She had finished her college course work several months ago and stayed on at the camp. Sometimes at night she lay awake chiding herself for her inability to make a choice and move forward in her life. With school behind her, nothing really held her to the small town of St. Mary's and this camp that Dillon Graves was pouring his life into. Even in her foolish years she had had enough sense to major in business and economics; she was confident she could get a job if she wanted one. Yet she had been reluctant to leave. Something invisible, intangible held Jenna to the Homestead.

Stacie's voice brought Jenna back to the present. "I always imagined you and Dillon would get a little closer."

Jenna flushed. "We are close. We're good friends."

Stacie cocked her head. "You know what I mean. You two started hanging out together more than two years ago. . .about the time Brad and I got married."

Jenna was fumbling for words. "Well. . .we. . .I mean. . . ."

"Oh, never mind. I didn't mean to embarrass you. It's just that Dillon is such a great guy, and you've been a big help to him out here. Both of you have really poured your hearts into this place."

Jenna took advantage of the opportunity to change the subject. "Have you heard Dillon's latest plans? He's going to build a new set of stables and add some other farm animals." She laughed briefly. "He's even thinking of getting a couple of llamas."

"Llamas?" Stacie asked incredulously.

Jenna raised her eyebrows. "That's what he says."

"Well, Dillon Graves usually accomplishes what he sets out to do. He's sure got Brad sold on all the reconstruction he's planning. Brad's never home on weekends anymore."

"That's what you get for marrying a talented, generous carpenter."

"I don't mind really, as long as this is the project taking up his time."

"Speaking of those guys, do you think they've worked hard enough today to deserve any lunch?"

Stacie smiled. "They've sure made a lot of noise. They better have gotten something accomplished."

"I've got a stack of sandwiches in the fridge," Jenna said. "Do you think it's warm enough to eat out at the picnic table? Oh, will you be comfortable out there?"

Stacie waved away Jenna's concern. "I'll be fine. I put on a good show with my whale imitation, but I'm fine." To prove it, she put her feet solidly on the floor and, in a smooth motion, pushed herself out of the rocker. "See?"

"You'll get no more sympathy from me."

Jenna led the way to the kitchen. They picked up the tray of sandwiches, a jug of lemonade, and a plastic tablecloth and continued out the back door.

Although Brad and Dillon were nearby in plain sight, Stacie reached for the familiar mallet and swung it hard against the gong hanging outside the cottage, making Jenna laugh. The men pivoted and stared at her.

"Did you want to say something, sweetheart?" Brad said patronizingly.

"Lunch is served."

Jenna had spread the tablecloth over the wooden picnic table and now set the sandwiches in the center.

"We forgot cups," Stacie said. "I'll get them."

Stacie disappeared through the back door and Jenna sat down. She smiled at the sight of Brad and Dillon thundering over to the table and shaking it with their weight as they sat side by side on one bench. Dillon's hair, always curly, was an array of knots made even tighter by the humidity. His gray eyes flashed a smile at Jenna.

"Whatcha got?" Dillon asked.

"For you, chicken salad, no onion," Jenna replied.

He smiled at her. "You're pretty handy to have around here," he said, picking up a sandwich. "You're the only person I know who accommodates my dislike of onions."

Jenna turned her head away slightly so no one would see the color rise in her cheeks.

"Stacie always makes me eat all my broccoli," Brad whined playfully, just loud enough for Stacie to hear as she returned with the cups.

"I heard that. I want you to set a good example for the baby," she retorted.

"Is Doug gone?" Jenna asked innocently as she poured lemonade. "He usually says hello."

"Hm-mmm," Brad nodded, his mouth full of roast beef. "Said he had to get back. He'll be back out on Wednesday, though, with the rest of the load."

"Sounds like he needs a bigger truck," Jenna observed. "He's always coming out with only part of an order."

Stacie turned to Dillon. "Jenna tells me you're going to build a new stable," she said. "Is that a pretty big project?"

Dillon nodded and swallowed his food. "My goal is to re-place every building out here or remodel it enough to make it last another fifty years. We've done most of the cabins. . .with the expert help of your gracious husband. . .over the last couple of years. Now it's time to start on the other buildings."

"I haven't seen any flyers about the camps you're running this year. Are you doing the same as you did last year?" asked

Stacie.

Dillon nodded again. "Yes, weekend family camps and a few special events for some of the local churches. But by next summer we should be ready to swing into action and run week-long youth camps all summer long."

"Your financial backers have sure been patient with you," Brad observed.

"We ran weekend snow camps all winter. We take in enough on the weekends to make the banks believe that eventually we will be profitable."

"What about the scholarships you give?" Jenna asked. "Time and time again you tell someone who can't afford the fee that they can come to camp anyway."

Dillon shrugged. "The Lord provides. Let them come."

Jenna watched Dillon as he nonchalantly reached for another chicken salad sandwich and refilled his cup.

Dillon had gotten involved in the camp only because he had been working with Stacie at the time the church group had taken on the project. In those days, he had not even been going to church. Gradually he'd started joining their activities and eventually led the cause to save the camp from being bought up by a developer. Somewhere along the line, the camp had come to mean as much to him as it did to all the others. Now he spoke with such simple, unassuming faith that it almost brought tears to Jenna's eyes. Oh, to be that sure of things.

"I hate to eat and run," Brad said, swigging the last of his lemonade, "but we have to get back into town."

"But I have chocolate chip cookies," pleaded Jenna.

Brad resolutely shook his head. "No bribes today. Stacie has a doctor's appointment this afternoon and we're going to be on time."

"Well, that's different," Jenna said reluctantly. "I suppose I could give you one for the road."

"Where did I leave my tool belt?" Brad wondered aloud, running his fingers through his thick, dark brown hair.

Jenna went into the kitchen and took a clean plate from the cupboard. Absentmindedly and while eyeing the activity outside through the window, she arranged a dozen freshly baked chocolate chip cookies on the plate. Brad had found his tool belt and tossed it into the back of his work van. Jenna shook her head; how did Stacie ever manage to climb up into that van? She saw Brad smile at Stacie across the driveway and Stacie wriggled her fingers in response.

Three years ago, when Brad and Stacie had briefly broken their engagement, Jenna had devoted herself to attracting Brad's attention. But her overtures had been unsuccessful and now she was glad. It was plain that Brad and Stacie belonged together. Jenna was only glad that Stacie had not held a grudge and that the two of them had been able to become good friends.

Jenna took the cookies outside; with one arm around Stacie, Brad used the other to grab four cookies.

"Hey, I said one for the road," Jenna teased.

"It's a long road."

"Don't you ever feed him?" Jenna said to Stacie, who only looked at Brad and smiled as they walked together back to the van. Jenna looked on as Brad tenderly helped Stacie into the high passenger seat and closed the door securely. In a moment they were gone.

"Well, I guess that leaves just you and me," Dillon said behind her.

She turned to face him. She picked up the sandwich tray, now nearly empty. "Yep. I'm going to clean up and then I'll be back out to feed the horses." She paused for a moment.

"Just how big is the new stable going to be?"

Dillon smiled. "Do you mean, just how many llamas am I going to get?"

"I hear they're tall. Better make the roof plenty high." Jenna slung the lemonade jug over one arm and walked the few steps to the back door. By the time she turned around again, Dillon had already headed back to his work. She watched his contented gait as he turned the curve in the road and was out of sight.

As she washed the plate and set it in the dishrack to dry, Stacie's words rang in Jenna's ears. "I always imagined you and Dillon would get a little closer."

"Me, too, Stacie," Jenna thought aloud, "me, too."

two

The afternoon settled into the pattern of most other afternoons. In exchange for living on the camp property, which Dillon owned, Jenna performed a variety of routine chores: keeping the grass mowed on the main lawn and the meadow; looking after the horses; stocking the dining hall kitchen with the food they served campers on the weekends; coordinating the delivery of supplies and the schedules of the volunteers; keeping the financial books. Jenna had often complained that Dillon was too easy on her. Despite her small size and delicate appearance, she insisted that she was capable of much more strenuous work than what Dillon assigned to her. Day after day, no matter what the weather or temperature, she saw him laboring on one project after another; surely there was more she could do to make his work easier, even if it was just handing him a hammer that was out of reach.

He boxes me in, Jenna often thought. *We're friends, but he doesn't see me for who I really am.*

Jenna decided to leave the dishes till later and just added the lunch things to the pile in the sink. She tossed the dish towel on the counter and headed back outside. The heavy spring rains kept the rolling lawn thick and bright. Jenna thought she had never seen such a beautiful green—emerald and intense. She had mowed it only three days ago, but already it looked like it should be cut again, within another two days at the most. Dillon had indulged in a rider lawn mower that made the job quite easy. But Jenna would not have minded, anyway. She loved being outside; it was early enough in the season to be warm and inviting without the sticky heat she knew would arrive in a few weeks.

Spring at the Homestead brought everything to life. The bulbs she had painstakingly spaced around the cottage last fall had sprouted and bloomed into tall, luminous, yellow and red tulips. The enormous maple tree behind the cottage cradled a bird's nest high in its branches; Jenna had followed the movements of the mother bird for weeks as she lined the nest and sat on her eggs. The earth beneath her feet was rich and black and soft under her step. It was as if everything around the camp was bursting with the vision of what the place would be when the renovations were complete and the Homestead could operate at full capacity the entire year.

It was a dream Jenna had had for more than two years. She knew that it would be another year or two before the dream came to life the way the season around her had. And as much as she wanted to be present when it happened, she was not sure she would be. She did not want to be just tagging along for the ride. Dillon was being gracious about letting her live in the cottage, and she did perform legitimate duties for the privilege. But how long would that last?

How long should it last? she often wondered. The arrangement had been appealing while she was still in college. But she had finished her course work at the end of the January term. In a few more weeks, she would walk through the official graduation ceremony and then she would be facing the rest of her life. Shouldn't she do something more than feed someone else's horses and displace the rightful owner of that lovely stone cottage? Even if she wanted to stay, Dillon was probably expecting her to move on.

Dillon had asked her if she would stay through the

summer, when he knew the camp would be busy on the weekends. She had agreed immediately. But the fact that he had asked in the way he did—"through the summer"—impressed on her that he expected she would leave. Where would she go?

During the last few weeks, Jenna had been pondering her options more intensely. She could go home and live with her parents in Ohio while she tried to find a job. With a degree in business and economics, she was optimistic that she would be successful. Or she could try to stay in St. Mary's, although the town was small and opportunities were limited. And then there was always graduate school. She could get an MBA and put off facing the real world for another year or so. Rationally, and every day, she went through the list like a litany; emotionally she went through the wringer.

Why was it that some people were so sure of what God wanted them to do? Stacie had been so sure that God had wanted her to work at a new homeless shelter that she had almost lost Brad. Even Brad had been surprised that Stacie would let him break their engagement because he did not want her to move away for a new job. In the end, everything had worked out, but Jenna had never forgotten what Stacie had been willing to do because she was convinced of what God had wanted her to do.

Dillon had been just as sure that he was supposed to leave the homeless shelter to run the camp, and he had thrown himself into the task without looking back for even a moment. Fighting incredible odds, he had pulled the sinking camp from the snatches of financial ruin. Now, there was every reason to think the place would succeed.

For Jenna, God's Will always seemed like a murky, choking river that she was not sure she could cross.

Jenna headed down the path to the stable. The hill was so familiar that she hardly felt the incline anymore. At its crest, she loved to stand and soak in the beauty of the land around her. At the stable, eight sturdy horses, most of them new, grazed in the enclosed area. In the sun their coats shone with a healthy gleam. The manes that Jenna combed so meticulously fell around their heads with a gentle swish. With their tails they swatted at the flies, more every day. To Jenna it looked like a picture out of a children's storybook.

Eager for the distraction, Jenna swung her weight against the gate of the new fence Dillon had built last year and opened it. Inside the corral, she patted the rump of the nearest horse.

"How ya doin', Mandy?" she asked.

The horse neighed quietly and turned her head to nuzzle Jenna's hand, looking for an apple.

"Sorry, sweetie, I didn't bring any treats today. I'm afraid it's just plain old oats."

Jenna made her way inside the stable, ducking as she went through the door. The wood on one side of the doorway had started to rot years ago and the ceiling had never looked straight to Jenna. The walls of the cramped stalls had been adjusted to create more, smaller stalls. The stable was undeniably crowded. Though she was sentimental about the stable, Jenna recognized that it was time for a new structure.

She inspected the stalls where the horses had spent the night. Just as she thought, they needed cleaning out. She reached behind the door for the pitchfork and started the routine of freshening the hay. Unlike mowing the lawn, there was no easy way to do this job, but Jenna was grateful for the exercise it gave her. She hoped that the muscles that had developed in her forearms helped to dispel the notion that she was a delicate porcelain doll who could not dig in and help out when there was work to be done.

After a while, she moved back outside, squinting at the bright sun after having been working in the shadows of the stable. Heaving a fifty-pound bag of oats, she poured the contents into the food trough. She ran water into a second one. Without further urging, the horses meandered over and nudged against each other for the best eating spot. Jenna stood nearby, contentedly watching the animals eat, feeling satisfaction in the work she did.

Jenna looked at her watch. It was still only the middle of the afternoon and she was already done with what she needed to accomplish for the day. There was plenty of time tomorrow to work in the camp kitchen getting ready for the coming weekend. She could indulge in a leisurely long walk around the grounds before heading back to the cottage for an evening with a novel.

Being careful to latch the gate securely behind her, Jenna started out on a loop that had become a daily ritual. After the long winter, when just driving into town and back was strenuous enough, she was glad for the opportunity to walk the grounds every day, noticing the wildflowers and creeping ground cover along the path and hearing the frogs croaking in the pond. With spring just about over and summer around the corner, the trails were dry enough that she could choose any of them to hike. Occasionally she took one of the horses, but generally she preferred to be on her own two feet.

She chose a path that cut through the center of the camp. It was a heavily wooded trail; Jenna almost could not see the sky through the towering trees bursting with new foliage. Even in the middle of a summer day it was dusky and cool on that trail. But she knew it would eventually empty out into the broad meadow on the other side, and that was one of the reasons Jenna liked to walk it. She was strongly drawn to this trail on the days that she wrestled the most with the decisions she faced in the next few months. It was almost as if she believed that one day as she emerged from the dank woods into the open sunlit meadow, she would also stumble on the light she needed to make her choice.

As Jenna walked the trail, she had to concentrate on her steps. Rocks and muddy patches and tree roots were common, and the soles of her white tennis shoes had long ago become slick and smooth. More than once she had fallen on this trail. Still, she returned to it over and over again. It was a good place to think.

Her mind went back to Stacie Davis. Three years ago, Stacie had taken a challenging new job, a job she had had her sights set on for years. Then she got married; then she and Brad bought a house; now she was having a baby and talking about cutting back on her job. From Jenna's perspective, Stacie's life was one major change after another, and she often wondered how Stacie managed to stay so calm and collected through it all. Of course it helped that she had Brad, who was solid as a rock.

During her fleeting flirtation with Brad three years ago, Jenna had seen just how solid Brad was when it came to Stacie. There was no changing the way he felt about her. That had to mean something to Stacie when yet another upheaval came into her life. But Jenna suspected that even without Brad, Stacie would stay steady on a roller coaster. What amazed her most of all was that Stacie had made an effort to become her friend despite Jenna's puppy dog crush on Brad.

Jenna could not imagine such a sense of security. She could always get a date when she wanted one, but more and more she was tired of dating. Nothing ever seemed to lead to what she wanted. While her friends graduated from St. Mary's College and moved on, Jenna seemed trapped in a time warp, unable to step forward. It just seemed easier to settle into the routine at the camp, including a comfortable but unpromising relationship with Dillon Graves. That was a security of sorts, she supposed.

Or maybe the problem was that she did not know what she wanted and that the camp routine and the remote location of the Homestead kept her from having to face the unknown and discover what lay ahead. Dillon certainly did not have that problem. To everyone's utter shock, he had left a promising career in social work, a job that he loved, and stepped forward into the era of the Homestead.

At first the camp was going to be a side project; Dillon kept his job and lived in town. Jenna was already living on the grounds looking after what little there was to do back then. When Dillon decided he wanted to invest all his time in the camp, she had immediately prepared to move. She assumed he would want to move into the cottage, as he had every right to do. But he had insisted that he still needed her there and that he would be quite content with renovating one of the cabins. "A little updated plumbing, some electricity, and I'll be fine," he had said last year and promptly moved into a two-room cabin. Brad had helped him to add a small kitchen and rewire the building. Dillon seemed truly content.

Still, Jenna felt that she lived at the Homestead on Dillon's indulgence. She loved it there—the beautiful outdoors, the animals, even the crowds swarming around on the weekends. She truly loved it.

But she did not belong, not in the sense that she felt she could stay indefinitely. Jenna had helped to raise some of the money to keep the place going, but it was Dillon who had risked everything he had financially. It was Dillon who would never see the economic light of day if the camp did not start turning a profit within the next couple of years. The property belonged to Dillon, and Jenna was not sure she would ever feel that she belonged. Eventually she would have to move on, as frightening as that was.

Although she knew that Dillon could easily replace her, Jenna was glad he wanted her to stay the summer. She would savor every moment of it, every image of beauty that the long days provided.

The trail ended and she came out into the meadow, as she knew she would. Across the field, she could see Dillon working on something outside his cabin. He was bent over a pair of sawhorses, thoroughly absorbed in whatever he was doing. Jenna could not see what it was. She paused for a moment in the middle of the meadow as she considered whether to disturb him. It was tempting. She knew him well enough to know that he would not be annoyed by the casual encounter. Although they lived quite separately on the camp grounds, it was not unusual for them to come upon each other and settle into an amiable conversation on some neutral topic.

But Jenna turned and walked away from Dillon's cabin, back toward the main entrance and the stone cottage and her waiting novel.

three

Jenna nearly lost her balance when the busboy bumped her elbow with his loaded tray. Thinking that he would mumble an apology over his shoulder, her eyes followed him as he kept walking. But he seemed not to have noticed the collision or was so accustomed to such incidents that he did not think it warranted an apology. It was innocent enough, she supposed. The restaurant was busy and the cramped waiting area was filled beyond capacity. The overflow was clearly clogging the walkway that the staff used between the kitchen and the dining room. Jenna's group of nine had already waited more than half an hour for a table.

It had become a first-Sunday-of-the-month ritual and it was like this every month—crowded, noisy, stuffy. But the group from the college and career Sunday school class came anyway on the first Sunday of every month. Sunday school, church, out to eat—very predictable. St. Mary's did not offer too many choices in restaurants and months ago the group had quit looking for better options and settled for O'Reilly's. The food was superb and smaller parties were seated efficiently. But their group, which ranged from eight to fifteen at a time, always waited a long time for the restaurant staff to push together enough tables to accommodate them. Today was no different. But today Jenna wondered why she put herself through this. She did not have to do it just because the rest of the group did.

And her feet hurt. Since she had been living at the camp

and wearing tennis shoes most of the time, her feet were not used to the dress shoes she jammed them into on Sundays.

Jenna was grumpy, no doubt about it. She saw a spot on a crowded bench open up and dropped into it quickly and gratefully. Immediately she realized Stacie was still standing and tried to get her attention. She would willingly give up the seat for her pregnant friend, but Stacie was engrossed in a conversation and did not notice Jenna's efforts. Oh well, Jenna thought, sighing. I might as well enjoy it. She leaned back on the cracked vinyl bench and felt her hair get pinched in the ripped upholstery.

"Ouch!" she muttered under her breath, leaning forward again and smoothing the back of her head.

Finally the loudspeaker cackled and a weary voice said, "Davis, party of nine. Davis, party of nine." Jenna got up and trailed after the group to their tables at the rear of the restaurant.

"At least they didn't try to make us squeeze into a booth this time," someone said.

"Are you nuts? Nine people in a booth?"

"More likely they took one look at Stacie and knew she'd never get out again."

A general chuckle rippled through the group. Brad and Stacie had been the first ones to get married and now Stacie was the first to be pregnant. Every week someone had a new pregnant joke. Stacie took it all in stride.

"I almost didn't get out last week," Stacie admitted. "I was getting some pretty funny looks from the waitress."

"Aw, I'm sure she's used to it. You and Brad have been coming here for years. It's probably not the first embarrassing moment you've had here."

"You're right about that," Brad agreed and went on to tell

the story of the first time he had kissed Stacie publicly in the restaurant and how she had blushed deeply.

Jenna had heard the story before and her mind wandered. The plain fact was that she was not in a very good mood. Outwardly she appeared even tempered, though perhaps quiet at times. Everyone thought she was steady as a rock. If only they knew the truth. Inwardly she could tie herself into a knot over practically nothing, and it had happened again last night.

When the last of the Saturday campers had left and the grounds were once again quiet, she had seen Dillon out cleaning up litter and emptying trash cans. She had gone out to help and the job was soon done. Throughout the process they had chatted amicably as they had always done. Then on an impulse she'd invited him into the cottage for a late, light supper. Without a moment's consideration, he had turned her down. When she had looked at him, no doubt with surprise on her face, he had simply said that he had some other things he needed to take care of and maybe they could do it another time. He had turned and walked away, pressing his lips together as if deep in thought. In fact, thinking back on the day, Jenna realized Dillon had been withdrawn and isolated most of the day. Jenna had been too busy to notice earlier.

Jenna had no reason to feel the way she did, and she knew that. If Dillon was busy, he was busy. Hers had been a last-minute invitation; it should not have surprised her that he had already made plans. Nevertheless, she felt rebuffed and was annoyed. Why couldn't Dillon see who she really was? Why couldn't he recognize what it meant to her to invite him for supper.

"Jenna?"

The person next to her nudged her elbow and she jumped slightly. "Pardon?"

"Paul asked about Dillon. He wasn't in church today. Where is he?"

Jenna swallowed the irritation that rose up inside her and answered as pleasantly as she could. "I don't know. He didn't say anything to me."

It was the simple truth. She wished everyone would quit thinking that she knew about everything Dillon did. What other conclusions were people jumping to about her relationship with Dillon?

The conversation drifted away from Jenna again.

"When are you quitting work, Stacie?" Donna asked.

"I'm going to work right up until the baby comes."

Brad was shaking his head. "I can't convince her to let go a little early and get off her feet for a few weeks."

Stacie rolled her eyes. She and Brad had had this conversation a dozen times. "There's too much work to do, and no one to do it. I want everything to be caught up by the time the baby comes. I'll be off for three months then."

"Aren't you quitting?" Donna probed.

"Not completely. I want to stay on part time."

"But doesn't your position require someone to be there full time?"

"That's part of the problem that Brad refuses to understand." She glanced over at her husband. "There isn't anyone else. The board is looking for a replacement now."

"They don't have much time to find and train someone."

"I know. I'm getting a little nervous about it. I've put out a lot of feelers, too, but so far we just haven't found anyone."

"What about Dillon? Wouldn't he consider coming back for a little while, in a pinch?"

"I think the board has already thought about that. But he doesn't really feel like he has time."

"Looks like he doesn't even have time to come to church," someone interjected.

"Oh, lay off of Dillon," Brad said in his friend's defense. "He's a grown man. He can decide whether he wants to come to church."

Jenna listened to this whole interchange as an outsider. Periodically she wished she had not come at all today, not in the mood she was in. But she was here and they had ordered lunch and she could not find a suitable excuse to leave just yet. When their food came, she ate steadily and only spoke when someone said something directly to her. One part of her brain chided her for her mood; the other side slid deeper and deeper into depression.

After a while the conversation was too much for her; the group was too much. She needed to be able to think. Having finished most of her lunch, she set her fork down.

"I've got to get back to the camp," she said with a false brightness, laying some money on the table for her meal and slipping into her linen blazer.

"I thought you had volunteers looking after things today," Stacie said.

"I do, but something always comes up."

"Well, maybe Dillon is there. Why don't you stay for some coffee?"

Jenna knew Stacie had perceived her bad mood and wanted to help her out of it. "Thanks anyway, Stacie, but I really think I'd better be going."

"Come by the house this week. You've still never been out there. You can see the nursery."

Jenna nodded. "I'll call you."

❧

Forty minutes later Jenna pulled her used red Chevy station

wagon through the main gate at the camp and slipped into her reserved parking spot in front of the cottage, relieved to be on her own territory again. The camp had been busy on Saturday, but only a church high school youth group remained overnight. Some of the kids were starting to straggle out of the dining hall to enjoy a couple of hours of recreation before boarding the bus for the ride home. Two of the boys saw her getting out of her car and flagged her down.

"The sports equipment shed is locked. Can you let us in?" they pleaded.

"Sure," Jenna answered. She juggled her Bible and her Sunday newspaper to fish in her purse for the ring of camp keys. Wishing she could at least have taken off her heels, she led the way down the narrow stone path to the shed behind her cottage and opened the padlock. The boys grabbed a couple of basketballs and a frisbee.

"Oh, I almost forgot. There was a guy here looking for you a while ago," one of the boys said.

"Mr. Graves?" Jenna speculated.

"No, I know who he is. This was somebody else."

"Did he say what he wanted?"

"No. Just said to tell you Doug came by."

"Doug? Doug was here?" The only Doug she knew was the lumber deliveryman. She realized that she did not even know his last name.

"Yep. But he said he couldn't stay." Having done his duty in relaying the message, the boy turned to go. Balancing a basketball on his finger tips, he said, "Thanks," before following his buddy back up the path.

Jenna let herself in the back doorway of the cottage and quickly changed into jeans and a light sweater. Her full, sun-lightened hair tied loosely at the back of her neck, she went back outside and crossed over to the dining hall to make sure everything was going well over there. To cut down costs, the group had opted to prepare their own meals, but she wanted to be sure they had found everything they needed.

"Everything okay in here?" she said, as she popped her head through the doorway to the big kitchen. She saw one of the counselors vigorously shaking her finger.

"Sharon! What happened?" Jenna asked.

Obviously embarrassed, the counselor confessed, "I cut myself. Someone put a knife in the dishwater and I didn't know it was there."

"Then it wasn't your fault."

"But it's still my finger. I can't get it to stop bleeding."

Jenna pulled a stepladder over to one cabinet. "I told your youth pastor that there was a first aid kit up here."

Sharon shook her head. "He didn't tell me. I'm glad you came along when you did."

Jenna cleaned the cut and applied pressure to stop the bleeding. "With the blood out of the way, it doesn't look too bad." She bandaged it securely. "Here, I'll help you with the rest of the dishes."

"Thanks. I think I can still manage to dry." She took a fresh dish towel out of the drawer next to the sink.

"Have you seen Dillon?" Jenna asked casually.

"You mean the camp owner?" Sharon shook her head. "Not since breakfast. He checked on us then and said he'd be gone the rest of the day. He told us to find you if we needed anything else."

"Oh," Jenna nodded, though she did not understand Dillon's actions. "He didn't say where he was going, I suppose."

"Sorry. We assumed he was going into town for church."

"Well, if so, he never made it."

"I hope everything's okay," Sharon said.

Jenna was quick to reassure her. "I'm sure everything's fine. He's been pretty busy lately. He must have had something he had to do today." She pulled the plug out of the drain. "Well, we're done here. I hope you can enjoy the day a little bit before leaving."

Sharon laughed nervously. "You should see the cabin I was in with the girls. Looks like a tornado hit."

Jenna added her mild laughter. She did not tell Sharon that only three years ago the camp had really been struck by a tornado and that the cabin next to hers had collapsed in the powerful wind.

"I hope the group enjoyed their time here and that they'll come back again."

"I'm sure we will," Sharon said as they left the kitchen together.

❧

Three hours later, the group loaded up their bus and left for home. Jenna was left with the evening quiet and two mysteries: where was Dillon, and why had Doug come to the camp looking for her on a Sunday afternoon? She went through the routine of caring for the animals and then walked the grounds making sure all the windows and doors were closed in the cabins and that the main buildings were locked. Even past supper time there was no sign of Dillon; when she came to his cabin the shades were drawn and there was no discernable activity within. His car was missing, too, so obviously he had not come back yet.

Where was he? Dillon was not obligated to Jenna in a strict sense, but usually he let her know his plans—even if just to be sure the chores at the camp would be covered. Lately, however, they saw less and less of each other. His mind seemed to be somewhere else much of the time—and now all of him had disappeared for hours.

This behavior was not like Dillon. If he had not told Sharon, the counselor, that he would be away, Jenna would be worried by now. One last time, she looked at the stillness of his cabin.

Jenna meandered back to her own cottage, picking up odd bits of trash as she went along. Under the trees, darkness had already arrived, but she knew the way well. Back in her own cottage, she warmed up some soup for supper and settled down to read every page and every advertisement of the Sunday newspaper that she had brought back from town. But she did not really care about the dollar sale at the local discount store. As she perused the paper, she kept her ears cocked for the sound of Dillon's car. He would have to pass by her cottage to reach his cabin. Most likely he would not stop, but at least she would hear him come in.

Eventually she stretched her feet out on the love seat and turned on the television. She dozed off without ever hearing his car.

four

It was not until Thursday that Jenna followed through on her promise to call Stacie. To her surprise, Stacie answered the phone at her desk on the first ring, then immediately insisted that Jenna should come by the house late that afternoon and stay for supper. "You can help me pick out wallpaper for the nursery," she pleaded. "Brad is absolutely no help."

So at four-thirty, knowing that Stacie would just barely have gotten home herself, Jenna pulled up in the driveway of the Davis' new house. They lived in an unfinished subdivision located halfway between Weston, where Stacie worked, and St. Mary's. From the Homestead, it took Jenna most of an hour to make the drive. She had not been off the camp grounds since Sunday.

Dillon had returned in the middle of the day on Monday and resumed his activities as if he had done nothing unusual. He volunteered no explanation for his absence and Jenna did not feel free to probe for one. On Tuesday Jenna mowed the back meadow and Dillon brought in an architect to finalize plans for the new stable. On Wednesday he casually asked her if she thought the dining hall needed a fresh coat of paint. So for three days they had continued their routine undisturbed. It was business as usual, only for Jenna the question mark over her life grew larger every day.

Jenna shut off the engine and pulled the key out of the ignition. As she got out of her car, she looked dubiously at the scrawny trees and shrubs that passed for landscaping in new

construction areas. It seemed clear that some of the growth
would not survive. Fresh sod had just been laid in the front
lawn; the seams between the strips were still visible. Jenna
was so accustomed to the unhindered vegetation of the camp
grounds that the saplings looked pitiful to her, especially in
contrast to the artificially cultivated sod. She had a hard time
picturing what the neighborhood might look like in twenty
years when the lots were filled in and the trees fully grown.

Stacie and Brad seemed happy with their choice of a home.
Brad had done some of the interior carpentry work in several
of the houses on the block, and his relationship with the developer had resulted in a good price on the house that Stacie
and Brad had decided to purchase. Stacie was taken with the
idea of living in a house that Brad had worked on—at least
until the day came that he could build the dream house he had
been promising her for years. They had moved in five months
ago, shortly after Stacie had discovered she was pregnant,
and she had thrown herself into a decorating frenzy. Despite
the best intentions, Jenna had never made it out to the new
house before this. Her eyes absorbed every detail of the place.

Stacie was at the front door, open to the spring air, before
Jenna could ring the bell. "Hi!" she said, pushing the screen
door open for Jenna. "I saw your car pull up."

Jenna gestured toward the front yard. "It looks great."

"No, it doesn't," Stacie said, shaking her head. "You don't
have to say nice things just to be polite. You have to really
use your imagination, but in a few years it'll have a whole
new look."

Jenna shrugged. "Maybe I should come back then?"

Stacie smiled pleasantly. "Don't be silly. Let me show you
around."

Stacie led Jenna out of the small entryway into the living

room off to the right. It was a good-sized room with an appealing bay window, and it was adjoined by a formal dining room that still stood empty.

"First the baby, then the dining room furniture," Stacie explained.

"Of course. Priorities. I hadn't pictured such big rooms," Jenna commented. "I guess I've gotten used to that little cottage where everything is so—"

"Convenient?" Stacie supplied. "I know what you mean. Wait till you see the kitchen." She led the way once more.

Jenna stood in the doorway and looked around. Stacie had obviously been hard at work in this room. An intricate, tricolored, stenciled border ran around the entire room just below the ceiling, and the same pattern was carried through on most of the cabinet doors. Color-coordinated dish towels hung next to the sink; matching potholders were above the porcelain basin. One corner of the room jutted out into a cozy breakfast nook that contained a small wooden table. From there the kitchen blended into an open family room area. A large wedding photograph hung over a fireplace. A door on the far side of the kitchen led out into the hall they had started in and where uncarpeted, polished oak stairs led to the four bedrooms upstairs.

"Come on," Stacie said eagerly, "let's go upstairs. I haven't done as much up there, but you can still look around."

They poked their heads into two bedrooms that held only unpacked boxes, took a look at the master bedroom, and then Stacie proudly opened the door to the nursery.

Jenna ran her hand along the smooth white rail of the new crib. It still had that store-fresh smell. A matching dresser and changing table stood on the opposite wall. "This is really pretty furniture," Jenna said sincerely.

"Do you like it? I'm glad."

"Don't you?"

"Of course I do, but with all the other expenses for the house, I was expecting to get second-hand furniture for in here. But Brad's mother insisted on furnishing the baby's room."

Stacie crossed to the dresser and opened a drawer. "She sent the most adorable sleepers." She pulled one out and held it up.

"It's so tiny!" Jenna exclaimed. "I love the fuzzy cow on the sleeve."

"The others have a lamb and a duck. I think I'll bring the baby home in one of them."

"That'll make your mother-in-law happy." Jenna looked around at the walls. "What colors will you use in here?"

"Picking out colors for a nursery is just about as hard as picking out names for the baby!" Stacie answered. She reached for a book of wallpaper samples. "Here, you can help me make a final decision. I have it narrowed down to these."

Jenna looked at the three choices Stacie had picked out: bunnies in pastel greens and yellows, bears with red or blue neckties, or balloons in primary colors. "They're all really cute," Jenna said.

"I told you that you don't have to say nice things just to please me," Stacie insisted. "Which one do you really like?"

Jenna hesitated for just a second and then put her finger on the balloon pattern. "This one. I've never known a kid who didn't like balloons. And I think the baby will like the bright colors."

"Then balloons it is," Stacie said with finality and closed the book. "I'll order it tomorrow."

Jenna was stunned. "You're really letting me pick the

wallpaper for your baby's room?"

"Why not? I trust your judgment."

"Stacie, I don't. . . ."

"What is it, Jenna?"

"It's just that. . . . Why do you go out of your way to be friends with me?"

"Why shouldn't I?" Stacie seemed genuinely puzzled.

"I don't know. I just feel on the outside of things so much of the time. It's hard to explain."

"Jenna, a lot of people really appreciate you. . .and everything that you've done for the camp in the last couple of years."

Jenna felt a blush coming on. "I know the reputation I have. A lot of people don't take me seriously."

"I don't know what you mean."

"Come on, Stacie, I've heard every dumb blond joke there is."

"Jenna! No one thinks you're a dumb blond."

"No one?" Jenna was unconvinced. Her jaw was set for an argument.

"Well, I confess that when I didn't know you very well I . . . . But that's ancient history. Brad and I think the world of you now. So does Dillon."

Jenna rolled her eyes and huffed. "Dillon doesn't even know I exist, Stacie."

Stacie sat down in the white wicker rocker next to the crib, the sleeper still in her hands. "Jenna, what has come over you? Dillon talks about you all the time. He works with you every day. You helped to raise the money to keep the camp open. You've been living in the cottage for almost two years. He depends on you."

"He's just used to me."

Stacie did not seem to know what to say.

"Dillon still doesn't know who I am," Jenna continued. "He doesn't talk to me, not really."

"I always thought you and Dillon were getting along great."

"We are. I mean, we don't argue or anything like that. It's just. . . ."

"Not enough anymore?"

Jenna could not hold back the blush any longer. "Yes," she said quietly, looking down at her hands. "He thinks I'm a child. . .a mature, responsible one, but a child nonetheless."

"Aren't you jumping to conclusions?" Stacie countered. "It's true, Dillon is older than you are—"

"Thirteen years, to be precise." Jenna fidgeted with a loose tag on the crib mattress. Her voice grew quiet. "I think he feels that gap every time he looks at me."

Stacie started rocking, not knowing what to say. "Even I did not know how you felt." She paused. "I understand your feelings, Jenna. Dillon is a wonderful man. There was a time that I. . . ."

Jenna laughed nervously and twisted a strand of hair around one finger. "I know. He was pretty taken with you."

It was Stacie's turn to blush. "That was a long time ago," she said, getting up abruptly. "Don't make more of it than it really was. I was on the rebound because Brad and I were having a hard time."

"But Stacie, haven't you noticed that Dillon hasn't really dated anyone since then? He always goes out with the group, but he never sees anyone alone."

Stacie blew out her breath and let her shoulders sag. "I guess I never really thought about it. Besides, he's busy. Renovating that camp is an enormous project."

"Of course it is," Jenna was quick to agree.

"But you don't think that's the only reason?" Stacie asked.

Jenna shrugged.

A mischievous look crossed Stacie's face. She stopped rocking and stood up. "I could talk to Dillon for you."

"When I was twelve I had a friend who said the same thing about a boy I liked. She gave him a note that was totally embarrassing."

"Oh, but I'm way beyond twelve. No notes."

"Don't be ridiculous. This is not junior high school."

"No, no, it wouldn't be anything like that." Stacie started pacing around the room. "I'd be so smooth he would never know what hit him."

"Please, Stacie. I wasn't trying to get you involved in this."

"I know. But you've opened up a whole new perspective on things for me. It's a challenge. I can't resist it."

"That's the last thing you need." Jenna tried to sound lighthearted. "You're having a baby in a few weeks, and they don't have anyone to take your place at work, and you have a new house to look after. You're not exactly lacking in challenges."

"Ah, but this would be different. It's a different sort of creative twist."

"I think you mean sneaky."

"What he doesn't know won't hurt him."

Jenna grew serious again. "Really, Stacie. I don't want to manipulate Dillon. There was a time that I would have, but not anymore. Besides, if I leave in the fall I'll probably get over this feeling anyway."

"Leave? What do you mean, leave? Where are you going?"

Jenna turned her palms up in a questioning gesture. "Out into the real world."

"What's wrong with the world you have now?" Stacie

tucked the sleepers back into the drawer and slowly walked toward the door. Jenna followed her out of the room.

"Nothing," Jenna said. "But my deal with Dillon was that I would live at the camp and help out while I finished school. Next week I graduate."

"Surely he's not asking you to move out," Stacie said, leading the way back down the stairs.

"No, but I think he's expecting it. At the end of the summer."

"Mmm. . . ."

"Stacie," Jenna said with a warning tone.

"Is your family coming for your graduation?" Stacie changed the subject quite deliberately.

Cautiously, Jenna took the bait. "My parents are. My brother could not get off of work."

"You haven't seen them since Christmas, have you?"

"No, and I'm looking forward to the visit."

"It'll be nice for you to have them there for that day."

Stacie grew quiet and Jenna knew she was thinking of her own mother who had died before seeing her daughter graduate from college. They wandered back to the kitchen just as Brad came through the back door.

"Hi, honey," Stacie said, offering her face for a kiss.

Brad obliged her and then patted her belly. "How's the little guy today?"

"Busy as ever. One of these days *she's* going to break one of my ribs during *her* gymnastics routine."

"Oh, *he* would never do anything to hurt *his* mommy."

Stacie gave a playful grimace at Brad's emphatic use of the male pronoun.

"I asked Jenna to stay for dinner," she told him.

"Sounds great. Who's cooking?"

Jenna laughed. "Don't get any ideas about my culinary skills. Haven't you noticed I always serve sandwiches or soup at my place?"

"But you cook for the campers sometimes," Brad retorted, handing Jenna a saucepan.

"This will never do. All my recipes serve a hundred people."

"So, we'll invite a few more people."

Stacie rescued the saucepan from Jenna. "I will cook. It'll give me a chance to think."

"About what?" Brad opened the refrigerator door and extracted a can of pop.

"Oh, I have some strategies to develop."

Brad popped the lid of the can and leaned back against the counter. "I thought we agreed you would leave your work problems at the office."

"I have. This is personal."

"Oh?"

Jenna did not know whether to stare at Stacie and silently plead with her to change the subject or to nonchalantly look around the room and pretend she was not hearing this conversation.

"It's nothing you need to get involved in, sweetheart. You go get cleaned up."

"Girl stuff, huh?" Brad didn't move.

Jenna blushed, but fortunately no one was looking at her at that moment.

Stacie gave Brad a shove. "Go take a shower. You stink."

To Jenna's relief, Brad left this time.

five

Stacie pulled open the refrigerator door and started rummaging around. "I know there are some chicken breasts in here somewhere. I just bought them."

"What can I do to help?" Jenna offered.

Stacie found the chicken and set it on the counter. "Well, you can tell me if you'd rather have potatoes or rice."

"That's easy. Potatoes."

"Mashed or baked."

"Mashed."

"When I ask Brad what he wants, he just says, 'Whatever, it doesn't matter.' It's nice to see someone who knows what they want."

"Well, when it comes to food, I suppose I do." Jenna's voice trailed off. If only the other choices she faced were as simple as potatoes or rice, mashed or baked.

Diverting the conversation from her own circumstances, Jenna asked, "What do you hear from Megan?"

"Not nearly enough, that rascal."

"But she and Rick are happy out in Arizona?"

Stacie nodded and continued eagerly. "She writes glowing letters about Rick's development project." She turned back to the chicken. "It's been more than a year since she got married and moved out there. I miss her every day."

"Maybe you could go visit after the baby is born," Jenna suggested. "I'm sure Megan would like that as much as you would."

The doorbell rang.

"Can you get that?" Stacie asked. "Brad's in the shower and by the time I waddle out there, they'll leave."

"Glad to." Jenna retraced her steps down the hall and pulled open the front door. She found herself looking through the screen at Dillon Graves.

"Jenna! What are you doing out here?" he said.

"Having dinner. What about you?"

"I wanted to talk to Stacie and show her some things."

"She's in the kitchen."

Jenna opened the door and let Dillon in, and he followed her back to the kitchen.

"Look what I found on your front step," Jenna said brightly.

"Hey, Dillon," Stacie said. "What are you doing here?"

"I've got a resumé I wanted you to see."

"You drove all the way out here to show me a resumé? Last I heard, the U.S. Postal Service was still in business."

Jenna chuckled at the bantering that was typical of Stacie and Dillon. His ability to keep pace in this kind of playful interchange was one of the things she found most appealing about Dillon. She liked to watch it.

"This is no ordinary resumé." Dillon smiled broadly. "This is the answer to your dreams."

Stacie gave a mock gasp. "You're coming back to work at the shelter?"

Dillon waved her away. "The next best thing. Sarah Martyn is available."

"Who's Sarah Martyn?" Stacie put down the knife she was holding and wiped her hands on a towel. She reached for the resumé.

Jenna looked on as Stacie and Dillon stood side by side, their heads together, looking at the papers. Her sleek, always neatly combed coppery hair contrasted with his rumpled curly mop perpetually in need of a trim.

"See? She's got six years experience in a similar facility," Dillon was saying. Jenna watched the blond curls at his temples shake ever so slightly as he spoke. "She wants to relocate to this area for personal reasons."

"Where did you find her?"

Dillon shrugged. "She's an old friend."

"Oh?" Stacie teased.

"She's an old friend who wants to make a change."

"An old friend who knew right where to find you?"

"Knock it off, Stace." Brad's voice preceded him into the kitchen. "Why do you always give Dillon such a hard time?"

Jenna laughed aloud. "As if you're any better!"

"I treat all people with the utmost respect," Brad said, tossing Jenna a potato. "Are you supposed to be doing something with these?"

"Dillon, can you stay for supper?" Stacie asked.

"I suppose so. As long as it's not that wicked chili that Brad makes."

"Nothing so exotic. Broiled chicken and mashed potatoes."

"Perfect."

"We missed you on Sunday," Brad said pointedly to Dillon, gesturing that they should sit down at the little table.

Jenna moved to the sink to peel potatoes but kept one ear bent toward the conversation between Brad and Dillon.

"I had to go out of town for a couple of days."

"Nothing serious, I hope."

"No, just had to see an old friend about a job."

So he had gone to see Sarah Martyn. Was it just about a job, Jenna wondered, or was there more to it than that. He had not gone to visit any of the other candidates for the job.

In fact, it really wasn't his problem, anyway. He no longer worked for the shelter. Why was he going out of his way to see Sarah Martyn?

Stacie finished seasoning the chicken and put it in the oven. Jenna filled a pot with water and set it on the stove so the potatoes could boil. For a moment she felt unsure of what to do next. She had finished peeling potatoes and had dropped them into the pot, but she did not want to go sit with Brad and Dillon. Relieved, she accepted a salad bowl and a knife from Stacie and started chopping vegetables. She was glad to be kept busy while she sorted out what was going on around her. She certainly had never expected to spend the evening like this—having dinner across the table from Dillon. His arrival had been innocent enough, and she supposed it would have been rude of Stacie not to invite him to stay for dinner, since it was obvious they were cooking.

Part of her was glad he was here. Maybe the four of them could relax a little bit and talk. They were away from the camp and she was determined not to have the conversation degenerate into camp talk. But could she keep Stacie and Dillon from talking about the shelter? Sarah Martyn was bound to come up again before the evening was over. She wished there was some way just to have a comfortable conversation among friends.

"I hope you both parked in the driveway," Jenna heard Brad say.

"Yes, sir, I did," Jenna answered.

But Dillon said, "I'm out front. Why? Is it illegal to park on the street?"

Brad laughed. "Not illegal; just dangerous."

"Get to the point, man," Dillon said insistently.

"The point is," Stacie interjected, "that you may have

noticed that we do not have curbs or sidewalks in this neighborhood yet. The ground out front is pretty soft."

"And if it gets wet—" Brad started the sentence.

"Like when Mr. Baxter turns on his sprinklers," Stacie continued Brad's thought.

Dillon stood up calmly and cooly. "Perhaps I should just go take a peek."

"Perhaps I should just come with you," Brad said.

They all went out the front door and looked in dismay at the sight of Dillon's car being sprinkled by the misdirected spigot in the next door neighbor's lawn. The ground around the car was quickly turning to mud.

"Better move it now, my friend," Brad said, giving Dillon a nudge in the back, "or you'll be here half the night waiting for a tow truck to come and get you out."

Dillon scowled at the prospect but complied. Ignoring the spray from the sprinkler, he opened the door and slid behind the wheel. The engine started. Unfortunately this was soon followed by the sound of a spinning rear tire. Dillon was already stuck. He shut the engine down before he made matters worse.

Jenna glanced at Stacie, and they couldn't help chuckling at the ludicrous sight.

"We'll have to help," Brad said. "Jenna, quit your snickering and get behind the wheel." Brad was already on his way out to the street. He pulled open the driver's door and motioned that Dillon should get out. "Let's push."

Jenna obediently positioned herself behind the steering wheel and inched the seat up slightly so she could reach the pedals comfortably. She rolled the window down and stuck her head out to see what the guys were doing. They were braced against the back left corner of the car, ready to push.

"Go!" shouted Brad.

Jenna accelerated, slowly at first, then a little more and a little more. Nothing happened except the groan of an engine working too hard and the whine of the tire still spinning. She could sense that the car was almost ready to move forward. Perhaps just a little more gas. It was worth a try. She pushed the pedal a little closer to the floor.

"Stop! Stop!" came the cries from the rear.

Jenna looked over at Stacie, still standing in the driveway, and saw her laughing wholeheartedly. What could be that funny?

Cautiously she opened the car door, leaned out, and looked back. She gasped and clamped her hand over her mouth.

Dillon was covered with mud from his neck to his knees. Brad had stepped out of the way in time, but Dillon had still been behind the car when Jenna had decided to give the accelerator one last push.

Quickly she got out of the car and, embarrassed, ran up the driveway to stand with Stacie.

"Stacie! Look what I did!"

Stacie was still laughing. "It's like watching an old slapstick movie. I didn't think things like that really happened."

"Oh, Stacie, I deserve all those dumb blond jokes! How could I have done something like that?"

"You were just trying to help."

"Yeah? Tell that to Dillon. Look at him."

Dillon had found a rag in the back seat and was trying to clean himself up as best he could. The sprinkler system continued whisking water at his car. He got behind the wheel himself again, while Brad stepped to the back bumper alone this time.

It took several more tries, but the two of them finally got

the car out of the mud and moved safely to the driveway.

"Come back in the house. I'll find you some clothes," Brad said.

Dillon did not say anything to Jenna as he walked past her and followed Brad into the house. Silently, she followed, with Stacie close behind her.

"The chicken!" Stacie cried as soon as she got in the house.

Jenna was surprised at how fast Stacie could move when there was a need to do something more than waddle. They got to the kitchen to find the chicken smoking from the broiler and the potato water completely boiled away. Jenna grabbed the pan and tried to stir. Lumps of soggy potatoes stuck to the bottom of the pan. Stacie set the chicken pan solidly on the counter.

"So much for dinner," Stacie said flatly, reaching to turn on the exhaust fan.

The evening was clearly deteriorating. Jenna was not sure what she wanted at this point—to leave and completely forget about the last half-hour or to stay and try to salvage some of the potential she had seen in the evening a few minutes ago.

"Maybe we can rescue it," Jenna said, poking at the chicken with a fork. It was blackened and tough. "Then again, maybe not."

"I think not," Stacie said.

"We still have the salad," Jenna said optimistically.

"Yes, and we could do some baked potatoes in the microwave, maybe whip up a cheese sauce to pour over them. And I think I might have a bit of chopped ham left."

"Let's do it." Jenna was momentarily encouraged that the evening would not be a complete disaster—though she dreaded the moment Dillon would reappear in the kitchen. She set about scrubbing the four biggest potatoes in the bag while Stacie hunted for cheese, butter, and milk in the refrigerator.

By the time Brad and Dillon returned, dinner was on the table. The baked potatoes and salad were supplemented by thick slices of french bread and some fresh apple slices.

"I see we've had a change of menu," Brad said, as he sat down. "Guess this just hasn't been our night."

Jenna turned to Dillon. "I'm so sorry. I just can't believe I did that. I know better, I really do."

"It's all right, Jenna," Dillon said.

"I really thought we were going to make it that time." Jenna could not seem to stop explaining herself. "I just thought I'd give it one more try."

"Really, Jenna. No harm done." Dillon gestured at the fresh clothes.

Jenna forced herself to stop talking. Dillon did not sound upset, that much was true. But he did sound vaguely distant from her. Could he really have dismissed the incident from his mind so quickly? Or was his mind on other things anyway?

Her earlier suspicions proved right. The dinner conversation was lighthearted for the most part, with an occasional reference to the missing chicken. But it was not long before the conversation circled back to Sarah Martyn and her qualifications to take over Stacie's position at the shelter in Weston. Dillon had already arranged for Sarah to come and meet with Stacie very soon, and Dillon assured Stacie that Sarah would be available to start work immediately if the board wanted to hire her.

As Stacie and Dillon got deeper into a conversation about the shelter's need for leadership, Brad got up and cleared the table and loaded the dishwasher. Jenna helped him, all the while keeping one ear tuned to the conversation at the table.

Brad said he had some paperwork to do and left as soon as the kitchen was cleaned up. Jenna made coffee and sat down at the table again with a mugful. After a while, though, it seemed clear that there was no real reason for her to stay any longer. Stacie had glided into a business mode and stayed there. The prospect of Sarah Martyn's coming to Weston had consumed the evening. Jenna had an hour's drive ahead of her, so she decided it was time to go.

Politely and as unobtrusively as she could, Jenna thanked Stacie for dinner and excused herself. As she did so, she saw Dillon look at his watch.

"I didn't realize it was getting so late," he said. "I'll be coming soon, too."

She smiled and nodded. "I'm glad you guys finally found somebody who is a real possibility."

She meant what she said. But there was more that she did not say—questions she did not dare ask aloud.

six

Jenna pressed her finger tips firmly against the stubborn red balloon in the bottom corner. This was the third time she had tried to get that edge of the wallpaper to stay in place.

"Stacie, can you hold this here?" Jenna asked. "The top keeps coming down when I work on the bottom."

Stacie lumbered off her stool and crouched in the corner to take hold of the dripping strip.

Jenna reached above her and gingerly straightened the top edge. With a sponge she made determined downward strokes, forcing the excess water out and pressing the wallpaper against the wall. "That's better," she said, satisfied that the strip would stay in place this time.

They both stepped back to admire the completed wall that had taken them most of the morning to cover. They had carefully trimmed around the window and tucked the cut edges behind the molding.

"Looks good, don't you think?" Stacie said.

Jenna nodded and inspected a seam between two strips. "Did we get those two close enough?"

Stacie peered at it. "I think so. It just looks funny because it's not dry."

"I've never done this before," Jenna said, with satisfaction in her voice. "It's kind of fun."

"I like seeing immediate results for my effort."

Jenna pivoted slowly and looked at the rest of the room. "However, we do still have three more walls, with a lot of stuff to cut around."

"Well, we may not get it all done today, but I'm glad we got started. I appreciate your help more than I can say." Stacie took off the rubber gloves she was wearing and dropped them on a lumpy heap in the middle of the room. They had pushed all the furniture together and draped a plastic dropcloth over the pile. "I don't know about you, but I could use a cup of tea."

Jenna, having been concerned all morning that Stacie was working too hard, was quick to take the cue. "Let's go downstairs and you can put your feet up for a while. I'll fix the tea."

Downstairs in the kitchen, Stacie gratefully sank into a chair while Jenna filled the kettle and put it on the stove to boil.

"The graduation was gorgeous," Stacie said. "We were all so proud to see you walk across that stage."

"Oh, thanks," Jenna said, embarrassed slightly. "And thanks for coming. I never expected so many people to come see me graduate."

"I'm only glad I could be there. Dillon hated to miss it."

"Did he?" Jenna could not help thinking that if Dillon had wanted to come, he would have. Instead, he had disappeared on one of the busiest weekends of the season.

If Stacie detected Jenna's skepticism, she ignored it. "You have to admit, it was a spectacular day for being outside. That's the sort of day that makes you believe summer is really coming."

"I know what you mean. I was actually sweating in that robe."

"Ah, yes, polyester. But you looked great."

Jenna reached into the cupboard for two mugs and the honey she knew Stacie would want for her tea.

"Even though I finished my classes in January, I didn't feel completely done with college until the ceremony. I didn't expect it to hit me quite like that. I really am not a student anymore."

"Well, the speaker gave such a rousing talk about the whole future being ahead and how you should grasp hold of what you want. It would be kind of hard not to be influenced by that."

Jenna smiled. "He was pretty energetic. But he almost made me more scared of the future, instead of excited about it."

"What do you mean?"

"I don't know how to do anything except be a student. What if I flop?"

"You won't. You're a college graduate, with the paper to prove it. Be proud of yourself."

The kettle whistled and Jenna filled the mugs with the steaming liquid. Stacie reached out to take her cup as Jenna sat down across from her.

"A college graduate who doesn't have a clue as to what to do next," Jenna said. "You always knew exactly what you wanted, but it hasn't been that way for me."

Stacie took a tenuous sip of hot tea. "I guess it always seemed clear to me what the Lord wanted, and I just did that."

"I want to know what the Lord wants," Jenna assured Stacie, "but somehow the lights are not coming on." She set her mug down on the table to let it cool. "My parents want me to come home to Ohio."

"Did they say that while they were here for your graduation?"

Jenna nodded. "In fact, I think they're assuming that I'm coming home after the summer. Mom's talking about painting my room and stuff like that."

"What do you think?"

"I've certainly thought about it. I'd have a place to live while I look for a job, so it has a certain amount of appeal."

"But. . . ."

"But, I'm not really close to anybody there anymore, except my family. So it would feel strange to move back. And I don't want to move back into the room I had when I was a little girl. I'm used to being in my own place."

"When you get a job, you could move out again."

Jenna rolled her eyes. "You don't know my mother. She tolerated my living on my own while I was in school, but I'm sure she thinks I should move back home and be happy there until I have a good enough reason to move out. . .like getting married."

Stacie added some honey to her tea. "Ah. I hadn't thought about it from that perspective. But I think you could stay where you are while you look for a job."

"At the cottage?"

"Sure. Dillon wouldn't mind having you around."

"Jobs are hard to get in a place as small as St. Mary's."

"You never know if you don't try. After all, I got a job in St. Mary's straight out of college. . . and so did Megan."

Jenna tilted her head thoughtfully. "Maybe if I started looking now I could find something by the end of the summer."

"Now you're talking." Stacie paused and stirred her tea before continuing. "Jenna, I have something to confess."

"What's that?"

"I talked to Dillon."

Jenna's eyes widened. "You talked to Dillon?" she echoed. She set her mug down a bit too hard.

Stacie put both hands up in a cautionary gesture. "It wasn't like that, I promise. In fact, I wasn't even the one who brought it up."

her usual thoroughness, she threw herself into preparation for it. Jenna nodded a lot, though she did not always understand what Stacie was talking about. Having a baby was so far removed from where her life was that she could hardly imagine that it would ever happen to her.

They worked the rest of the day in a comfortable companionship and got most of the room done. By the time she got in her car to drive home after supper, Jenna was aching from standing in awkward positions and was ready to take a long hot soak in the tub before going to bed.

ra

During the hour-long drive along the back roads of the county, Stacie's words rang in her ears: *Just talk to him, Jenna.*

What would she say? Something like, "I've had a crush on you for two years, and would you please pay some attention to me?" That would never do. Or would she come right out and ask about his relationship with Sarah Martyn? Was he glad Sarah might be moving to town for personal reasons? Or she could simply tell him in a businesslike way that she intended to enroll in graduate school and try to break whatever mysterious hold he had on her once and for all.

"This is nonsense," she said aloud, and slapped the steering wheel with her fingers. "I will not stoop to manipulation. We're adults. I don't want him if I have to trick him into a relationship."

On that note, Jenna snapped on the radio and turned up the volume. She let country western music—something she normally abhorred—fill the car till thoughts of her own situation had banished. She even found herself singing along with one tune. After that the time passed quickly and she pulled up in front of the cottage cheered up.

Once inside, she changed musical styles and began humming her favorite hymns as she ran the bath water as hot as she could tolerate it and lowered her aching body into the old-fashioned, clawfoot tub. With a deep sigh, she leaned her head back and closed her eyes. She stopped humming and enjoyed the silence. As her body relaxed, her mind turned to short prayers. *Lord, show me Your way. Lord, guide me through the maze.*

After a delicious forty minutes in the tub, the water had cooled considerably. As Jenna got out of the tub and reached for a towel, she thought she heard a noise outside. Standing perfectly still and dripping onto the rug, she listened again. Nothing. Relieved, she let her breath out and pulled the plug in the bathtub. It was probably just a rattling water pipe, she told herself.

She toweled off and wrapped herself in a cozy robe. She slid her feet into some slippers and, holding a magazine, she padded out to the living room.

Then she thought she heard a noise again, a car engine this time, driving away from the cottage. Cautiously she peered through the opening in the front curtains without parting them. She rarely felt in any danger out here, even though she was in a setting that was isolated for most of the week. Dillon was in and out through the front entrance of the camp to keep an eye on things. At least, that was what she always told herself. She watched the red tail lights disappear down the camp road. Must have been Dillon I heard, that's all, she told herself.

But something did not feel right. On an instinct, and with the chain still on, Jenna opened the front door of the cottage and looked out into the darkness. Then her eyes dropped down to the ground and she saw the package propped against the door post. Swiftly she unchained the door and opened it wide enough to retrieve the box and whisk it inside.

With the door locked once more, she turned the package in every direction. It was wrapped in plain brown packaging paper with no writing, no card. The box was small, only about six inches wide and nine inches tall.

Clearly it was meant for her, and she had seen tail lights drifting off in Dillon's direction. With sudden decisiveness, Jenna tore off the brown wrapper and opened the white gift box inside. With a gasp of delight, she lifted out a small, detailed, wooden carving of an owl. Dillon was one of the few people who knew she had started collecting owls. He had once teased her about whether some of the wisdom from her owls would rub off on her.

What was Dillon trying to say by leaving such a gift? Was he opening the lines of better communication? Was he trying to say that he had been paying attention to her after all?

Jenna took the owl into the bedroom and set it on the table at the side of the bed. That night, she slept more soundly than she had in a long time.

seven

Jenna put her Friday night supper dishes—along with her breakfast and lunch dishes—in the sink and started making a mental list of Saturday's chores. After only a moment she relented and reached for a pencil and paper; there was just too much to keep track of. One of the larger churches in the county had reserved the camp for an all-day outing for the entire congregation. By ten o'clock tomorrow morning there would be 300 people roaming the grounds of the Homestead. This was the biggest group Jenna had ever had to handle. Rationally she knew she had to take the same steps to prepare for any group, whether large or small, but still she felt nervous about this particular group.

Dining hall dishes, first aid supplies, saddles, sports equipment—she kept going over the list to make sure she had not forgotten something. Lost in thought about the next day, she did not even hear the car pull up in front of the cottage. A sharp rap on the wooden door startled her.

"Stacie!" she said, pulling open the front door. "What are you doing here?" She saw Brad's van parked nearby, the engine still running.

"Oh, Brad is doing an estimate on a job near here and I wasn't in the mood to spend Friday night alone at home. Sorry I didn't get a chance to call. Please, please, can I hang out with you?"

"It's no problem, but I'm afraid there's not too much excitement around here," Jenna said, laughing softly.

"Well, it's better than being alone." Stacie turned and waved at Brad, who took the cue and pulled away. Stacie followed Jenna inside the cottage.

"I guess I'm just bored and restless and ready to have this kid," Stacie said, sinking into the love seat. "I have to keep busy or I'll go nuts long before my due date."

"Well, if you're going nuts, you've definitely come to the right place."

"Are you really busy these days?"

Jenna brushed her bangs out of her eyes. "I have three hundred people coming through here tomorrow."

Stacie's eyes widened. "I hope Dillon plans to be around, too."

"Definitely. But I don't think he's here tonight." Jenna hesitated for a moment. "Actually I need to check on a few things around the grounds. Do you want to just wait for me here? I'll be back as quickly as I can."

Stacie leaned forward and pulled herself to her feet. "I'll go with you."

Jenna was not sure that was a good idea. "Are you sure you're up to it? Wouldn't you be more comfortable here?"

"Jenna, look at me," Stacie said flatly as she gestured toward her bulging midsection. "I'm way beyond comfortable. Comfortable is not even on the list of options."

Jenna couldn't help but laugh.

"I'd like the exercise," Stacie continued, "if you don't mind slowing your pace a little bit."

Jenna opened the door again. "I've got all night. Let's go."

The spring sun had not yet fully set. In its waning phase, it lit the air with a gentle, inviting hue. The retreating light sneaked through the leaves of the trees, now full and green with the promise of gentler summer days, and sprayed a dancing pattern of shadows on the path in front of them. The camp was quiet and restful, yet bursting with anticipation of what the next day would bring.

Jenna forced herself to take slower, shorter steps than usual as they followed the road past the first set of cabins. The slight rise in the road required extra effort for Stacie.

Out of habit, Jenna paused briefly to double-check the doors and windows. Technically none of the day campers should be in the cabins, but it seemed like every week someone found their way into at least one cabin. In the third cabin she found a stray sock that she wadded up and pushed into her pocket.

They continued around the loop to the stables. Stacie followed Jenna through the gate and then into the dilapidated inner area. The door frame seemed less straight every day, Jenna thought.

"Is Dillon going to tear all this down?" Stacie asked, looking at an overhead beam.

Jenna glanced around. "I think he plans to build a new structure on the other side of the corral and then tear this one down."

"I suppose the horses need a place to stay while the new stable is going up."

Jenna nodded and heaved a saddle off of a hook. She checked to make sure the parts were all there. A couple of weeks ago a child had fallen off a horse because the buckle on the saddle had come loose. Fortunately no one had been hurt, but it had frightened Jenna. Now she checked every strap of every saddle before each new group arrived. Then she rounded up the grazing horses and nudged them inside their stalls for the night. Satisfied that everything was as it should be, she led the way out of the stables and pulled the door shut securely behind them.

She turned to Stacie. "How are you feeling? I need to do

some things in the dining hall, but we could just walk for a while first."

"I'd like to," Stacie said. "Maybe the fresh air and exercise will help me get a decent night's sleep."

"How long will Brad be gone?"

"At least another hour, I would think."

They continued around the loop leisurely. For much of the time they didn't even speak. They were content to let their surroundings speak to them. An evening breeze stirred the tree leaves; squirrels scooted across the road; a chorus of frogs had organized themselves in the pond.

Abruptly Stacie stopped walking and put her hand on her abdomen.

"Stacie?" Jenna asked softly, trying not to be alarmed.

Stacie did not seem able to talk for a moment. Finally, she said, "A contraction, I think." She took a deep breath and blew it out.

"But it's not time!" Jenna protested.

Stacie scrunched her face up. "All I know is that that hurt." She looked ahead down the dirt camp road.

"Stacie, what should I do? We have to get back to the cottage. You can't have a baby out here in the woods. You can't have a baby in the cottage, either. You have to go to the hospital. Do you know where to get hold of Brad?"

Stacie managed to laugh nervously. "Slow down, Jenna. Let's take one thing at a time."

"Just tell me what to do."

"Let me lean on you. The pain is gone for now. Maybe there won't be another one."

"Then it wasn't really a contraction?"

"Oh, it was a contraction all right." Stacie took another deep breath and started walking. "Let's just concentrate on getting back to the cottage."

Jenna stepped up close to Stacie and put one arm out for Stacie to lean on. They were on the back side of the hill and would have to walk over the rise to get back to the cottage. She remembered how hard it had seemed for Stacie to get over the hill in the first place. How would she ever be able to get back now?

She chastised herself severely. She should have insisted that Stacie wait for her in the cottage. Or she should have put off her rounds until Stacie was gone. She could just have well have gone out with a flashlight later. Or the car—why hadn't they thought about taking her car down to the stables? The evening had been so pleasant that walking had seemed like the natural thing to do. Now it was starting to get dark, and they were half a mile from a telephone. At this creeping pace, it would be a long time before they reached the cottage.

Then it dawned on her. It wasn't too late for her to get the car.

"Stacie, I have an idea," Jenna said, scanning the immediate area. "Let's find a place where you can sit down, and I'll go for the car."

Stacie nodded as a shadow of pain passed over her face.

"Another one?" Jenna asked.

Stacie nodded. "I don't have a watch on, but it didn't seem like very long since the first one."

"What does that mean?"

"If the pains start coming regular and close together, it means I'm going to have a baby."

"Not here, you're not," Jenna said, determined. "I'm going to get the car and get you into town." She looked around again. "Here, sit on this log. It's pretty comfortable, actually. I've sat there myself a time or two."

Laboriously, Stacie lowered herself to the log and tried to shift her bulk to a stable position.

"Okay?" Jenna asked.

Stacie nodded.

"Okay, then," Jenna said, walking backwards. "I'm going. I'm going to run. I should be back in about ten minutes." She turned around and ran.

As much as she liked walking, Jenna had never liked running. Through her thin tennis shoes she felt every rock and root along the road, but she kept going. It was only half a mile; surely she could run half a mile.

Finally, she was over the rise and the cottage—and her car—was in sight. Grateful to be going downhill, she gave in to the pull of gravity and nearly tumbled down the hill. But she got there.

She ran inside the cottage, looking for her keys. They were not on the hook by the back door. She dumped the contents of her purse onto the kitchen table—no keys. Getting more nervous by the moment, she started moving everything in sight. "Think!" she demanded of herself out loud. "Where did you put your keys?"

Then she remembered—the pocket of the sweater she had worn in the early morning. She dashed into the bedroom and found the sweater strewn on the floor. The keys were there.

Jenna looked at a clock. She'd already been gone more than ten minutes. Taking the keys and casting the sweater aside, she ran outside to her car. Swiftly she got behind the wheel and inserted the key in the ignition. The engine groaned and Jenna felt the pit in her stomach deepen at the thought of the car's not starting. But it did start and she roughly backed it up and then went forward again up over the hill. The road was full of potholes, but she did not care. She could only think of Stacie up there, alone, in pain.

By the time she reached Stacie, she had been gone seventeen minutes. She screeched the car to a halt and jumped out.

"It's okay, Jenna," Stacie said, calmly.

"Yes, it's okay," Jenna repeated. "We'll get you to the hospital now."

"No, I mean I'm okay," Stacie clarified. "The contractions stopped when I sat down."

Suddenly Jenna felt like she hadn't breathed at all during the last seventeen minutes. With a heavy sigh, she sank down on the log next to Stacie.

"Are you sure?" Jenna asked.

Stacie nodded. "Yep. I've been fine since you left."

"But I don't understand."

"They said in our childbirth class that this might happen. False labor."

"False labor?"

"The contractions are real," Stacie explained, "but they stop if you change your position or activity."

"So when you sat down—"

"They stopped."

"Stacie Davis, you really scared me!" Jenna said, finally starting to relax. "I don't know anything about helping someone deliver a baby. Megan is the one who stays sensible during an emergency. I'm likely to fall to pieces."

"I sort of have my heart set on the hospital, too," Stacie assured Jenna.

"Let's get back to the cottage." Jenna stood up and offered a hand to Stacie.

Jenna drove back at a slower, gentler pace, glancing over at Stacie every few seconds to reassure herself that everything was really all right.

"Should we try to call Brad?" Jenna asked.

"I don't think so. I'm fine, really." She looked at her watch in the fading light. "Besides, he'll be here before too much longer now."

Back in the cottage, Jenna put the teakettle on the stove and insisted that Stacie prop her feet up on the ottoman in the living room. She had long ago released her mental list of chores to do that evening. She watched every expression that crossed Stacie's face and listened to every intonation, staying alert to any sign that Stacie was in pain.

But she truly seemed fine. By the time they had finished their tea, Jenna's heart had stopped racing and she was breathing comfortably. When Brad arrived, Jenna jumped in and gave him every detail of what had happened.

"That's it, Stacie," he said with finality in his voice. "No more going anywhere by yourself, especially not out here."

"But I'm fine, Brad," Stacie said in her defense. "Nothing happened."

"But it could have. I don't want you out here at the camp unless I'm with you. You need to stay close to the hospital."

Stacie grudgingly relented and acknowledged the sensibility of his edict.

Brad took Stacie, who looked drawn and pale despite her insistence that she was fine, and they left.

Jenna wandered back into the kitchen and stared at the pile of dishes in the sink. I'm such a procrastinator, she thought. Why do I let the dishes pile up for two days at a time?

She attacked the dishes vigorously, resolved that she would no longer procrastinate about housework—or making decisions. Jenna knew that no one was expecting her to learn all about childbirth and stand by in case Stacie went into labor at the camp. Still, she had panicked at the prospect of having to deal with that challenge.

Perhaps she did not know much about childbirth, but there were other challenges in her life about which she could do something.

"No more sitting around making lists of options," she said aloud. "From now on I make choices."

eight

That night Jenna slept soundly. She had stayed up late to finish getting ready for the busy Saturday ahead and, shortly before midnight, she had heard Dillon's car go past the cottage. But, instead of wondering where he had been all day, she stuck to her resolve to take charge of her own life and not make decisions based on what other people might want. Where Dillon had been all day was his business. She went to bed at midnight and slept solidly until six o'clock in the morning.

After a shower and a hearty breakfast—she knew she might be too busy to eat again until the evening—Jenna was ready to begin the day. She wore her most comfortable jeans and a deep green cotton knit shirt, clothes that would allow her to move about easily. At eight o'clock she pulled on a light windbreaker and went outside to meet the group of volunteers who would help her manage a crowd of nearly 300 people.

Right on cue, the minivan carrying eight volunteers arrived and parked outside the cottage. Most of them had been to the camp before and knew their way around and what their responsibilities would be.

"Any last questions?" Jenna asked, after welcoming everyone and giving a short pep talk.

"Did you ever find that big pot that was missing last weekend?" asked one of the kitchen crew.

"Under the sink."

"What about the new air pump?" someone else asked.

67

"In the equipment shed."

Gradually everyone dispersed to their stations, readying themselves for the two church buses that were due to arrive at nine o'clock.

They were right on time. Two reconditioned school buses, painted green, lumbered through the entrance, their drivers cautiously guiding their tonnage down the narrow driveway.

Jenna caught the eye of the first driver and waved her arms to indicate he should proceed to a larger parking area beyond the cabins. When the second bus had passed her, she followed as quickly as she could on foot.

Children and parents, teenagers and senior citizens tumbled out of the buses. Jenna sought out the church's fellowship coordinator, with whom she had been planning this day for several weeks.

"Did you get a final count?" she asked the harried young woman.

"Two hundred eighty-three, I think," came the answer. "We have only two buses, so a lot of people are coming by car. Should everybody park here?"

"Yes, please," Jenna said. "If that many cars are parked by the gate, there'll be a massive traffic jam."

"I'll find a couple of the high school kids to direct traffic and check in with you later." The fellowship coordinator turned to go, her eyes already scanning the crowd for the kids she had in mind.

"Just let me know if you need something," Jenna said before turning again to welcome more guests to the Homestead.

Throughout the morning the cars arrived. For many families it was the first recreational outing of the summer season. As Jenna worked and watched everyone all morning, she imagined how everything would look at the end of the summer. Winter white skin would be tanned and glowing. New tee shirts would be faded and rumpled. Laces would be missing from sneakers. Jeans would be exchanged for cutoffs. The meadow would have a well-worn path forming a baseball diamond.

"How ya doin'?" The voice behind her startled Jenna and brought her back to the beginning of the summer. She turned and saw Dillon grinning at her.

"Isn't this great? I love seeing so many people around here."

Jenna was quick to agree. "This is what it's all about."

"The horses are all out and saddled."

"Great. Thanks."

"I need to go out for a couple of hours, but I should be back before lunch."

"Take your time," Jenna said, forcing herself not to wonder where he was going on such a busy day. "Everything's under control."

"It always is when you're around."

Jenna blushed and looked away. "I'd better make sure the equipment shed is unlocked. I'll see you when you get back."

The awkward conversation came to a merciful end when a telephone began to ring. The bell on the outside of the dining hall reverberated throughout the camp. Everyone nearby turned their heads toward the jolting sound; a few even jumped slightly.

Jenna had long ago gotten used to the echoing bell. The phone also rang in her cottage, but since she was out and about so much of the time, she relied heavily on the outdoor extension. People who knew the camp well were patient enough to let the phone ring at least eight times.

From the parking lot, Jenna hustled down the path to answer the phone. A misguided driver was lost and needed help finding the camp. From there, Jenna walked up the path to the shed. One of the volunteers had already unlatched the door and was signing out equipment for various activities: basketballs, frisbees, horseshoes, softballs and bats, and volleyballs and nets.

"Everything okay here?" Jenna asked.

"No problems," came the confident answer. "Although some kids checked out the volleyball stuff, and I'm not sure they'll be able to get it up themselves."

"I'll check on them."

The kids, who looked like they were about ten or twelve years old, were on the front lawn struggling to attach the net to the poles that stood out there permanently. Even the tallest boy was not quite tall enough. Jenna fetched a stepladder and helped them get everything put together.

They quickly formed teams and took up sides. Jenna tossed the ball to one side of the net.

"Have fun," she said.

"I am."

For the second time that morning, Jenna was startled by a voice from behind. This one was familiar but she could not quite place it. She pivoted around to look.

"Doug? What are you doing here? Don't tell me you have a delivery to make in the middle of this chaos."

"No delivery," he said, laughing. "This is my church. I'm just here to have a good time like everyone else."

"I had no idea. You really go to this church?"

"All my life. Well, on and off, but I'm trying to get back into it."

"I didn't know you went to church." She gestured widely. "I think it's great you're here today. You'll get to see more than you usually do."

"I hope so. Hey, I know you're busy today, but I hope you can come watch the softball game after lunch."

"Oh, are you playing?"

"First base."

"I'll try to be there," she promised.

Although it was only midmorning, it was time to start working on lunch. Jenna crossed the lawn to the dining hall and poked her head into the kitchen.

"Everything okay in here?"

"Right on schedule," answered the woman doing the cooking.

"Did you find the big pot all right?"

The woman gestured with her head toward the stove. "Already got it full of chicken soup."

"Well, I guess I'll start setting the tables."

"There should be some folks here to help with that pretty soon, but they'll need to know where everything is."

"I'll just get things out and stack them on the push cart."

Jenna busied herself with finding enough dishes for the large crowd. In the past she had suggested to Dillon that they create needed storage space in the kitchen by getting rid of some of the dishes. But they had never had a crowd this big before. Right now she was glad that they had every bowl and dish in the cupboard. The piles filled the cart and overflowed onto the counter.

The dishes knocking against each other and the cook rattling around in the kitchen made just enough noise that Jenna did not hear the back door of the kitchen open. Pulling her head out of a lower cabinet, with her arms full of mugs, she almost fell into a tall, dark-haired woman. Though she was dressed casually, her makeup was impeccably applied and not a hair was out of place.

"Are you here to help with the tables?" Jenna asked.

"Pardon?" said the woman, confused.

"The tables. . . . Are you here to set them for lunch?"

"No, I—"

"She's with me." Dillon had come into the room. "I was just showing her around."

"Oh." This must have been the "errand" Dillon had had to do this morning. And maybe where he had been all day yesterday. And the reason he had missed Jenna's graduation ceremony.

"This is Jenna, my right hand here at the camp," Dillon said, putting a chummy arm around Jenna's shoulder. "And Jenna, I'd like you to meet Sarah Martyn."

Ah. This was Sarah Martyn. Awkwardly, Jenna emptied her arms of the dishes and extended her right hand. "I'm glad to meet you. I've heard Dillon talk about you."

Sarah smiled, showing bright straight teeth. A small mole on the left jawline was the only thing that kept her face from flawlessness. "Dillon talks about you a lot, too," she said smoothly.

Jenna laughed nervously. "Good things, I hope."

"Absolutely. He says he could never manage this place without help from someone like you."

Jenna nodded self-consciously. "I hope you enjoy your visit. Will you be here all day?" She hoped her question sounded innocent and casual.

Sarah nodded. "Till dinner time. Then Dillon will take me

back into town to meet Stacie Davis. I suppose you know her, too."

"Yes. You'll like her. Everyone does."

"I'm looking forward to meeting her."

"Well," Jenna said, leaning forward to load up her arms again, "I'd better get back to work. It takes a long time to set this many tables."

Dillon put a hand on Sarah's elbow. "I'm going to finish giving Sarah the tour," he said. "Then I'll be back to pitch in with things."

Jenna forced herself to smile. "I think everything's pretty much taken care of."

Eventually some real help for setting the tables showed up and the task went quickly. Dillon and Sarah did not return until it was time to serve lunch. Jenna had underestimated how many people they would need in the kitchen and had to pitch in herself with getting 283 people fed. While Jenna rushed around the kitchen, refilling serving dishes and answering questions—never having a chance to eat anything herself—Dillon and Sarah sat at a table eating, deep in conversation and seemingly oblivious to their surroundings. Jenna surmised that they were steeped in the intricacies of social work or the details of the job at the shelter, should Sarah decide to take it. Jenna was much too busy to really care what they were talking about, but it would have been nice to have had Dillon's help on the busiest day they had ever had.

Finally, lunch was over. Jenna was ready to sit down for a while, so when two o'clock came, she headed over to the meadow to watch the softball game. The teams had been determined ahead of time: under thirty and over thirty. People of all ages were playing, but mostly it was a group of men who might have been a little under thirty or a little over thirty. Doug was playing first base for the under-thirty team. Jenna found a spot along the first base line, spread a blanket on the ground, and got comfortable.

As the teams organized themselves, she was surprised to see Dillon playing on the other team. Sarah was seated along the third base line, directly across from Jenna. Dillon had changed into baggy shorts and a tee shirt with the sleeves cut off, as if he meant serious business in this game.

Dillon came to bat in the first inning. Jenna found herself almost staring at him as he set himself squarely in the batter's box and crouched in a stance that dared the pitcher to get the ball past him. He let the first two pitches sail past him, high and outside. On the third pitch, Jenna saw his forward foot lift slightly as he prepared to swing. The muscles in his exposed arms extended as he pulled the bat back and twisted his torso solidly against the ball. She heard the *thwack* of the bat and knew that he had hit the ball hard.

Closer to her, Doug sprang into motion. Diving deeply to his right, he stretched out his lanky form and got his glove on the ball just before it hit the ground, snatching a double away from Dillon. He tossed the ball back to the pitcher and grinned over at Jenna. She smiled back, and watched as Dillon and Doug playfully boxed each other at first base.

"You're too old for this," Doug said. "Give up now before you hurt yourself."

"You came pretty close to being on the same team," Dillon retorted. "Be careful what you say."

Dillon trotted back up the base line to stand with his teammates and the game resumed. Doug flashed another smile over at Jenna. The sun, high in the clear sky, was pleasantly warm. Jenna absentmindedly smoothed the blanket around her and turned her face into the breeze.

When it was time for the teams to change places, Doug jogged over to where Jenna was sitting and plopped down next to her.

"Hi," she said.

"Hi."

"Shouldn't you be over there?" she said, nodding toward home plate.

"I don't bat until the number seven spot."

"That was a good play."

"Thanks. I'm sure Dillon will try to retaliate, but it was fun."

For a moment they said nothing, watching the first batter take her place.

"Jenna?" Doug said.

She turned to look at him. "Yes?"

"I'd like to take you out sometime. Would you go out with me?"

Go out with Doug? Jenna had never even thought about that possibility.

"We could go anywhere you wanted," Doug said. "Dinner, a movie, bike riding. What would you like to do?"

Jenna hesitated. She really did not know Doug at all, except that he worked for a lumberyard and liked to tease Dillon when he made deliveries. And today she found out that he attended the church this group was from. But she liked him and enjoyed his quick visits when he made deliveries.

"Sure," she said impulsively. "I'd like that."

Doug popped up and looked toward his teammates. "Great. I'll talk to you later to see what you want to do."

Jenna looked across the field at Sarah Martyn. She followed Sarah's gaze and saw that she was watching Dillon out in right field. And he seemed to be looking back at Sarah rather than at the action of the game.

Yes, Jenna thought to herself, *going out with Doug is a good idea.*

nine

Jenna pulled a pink silk shell top over her head and tucked it into a pleated, flowered skirt. Her blond hair hung in loose waves around her shoulders; there was a bit of mousse in the bangs. As she applied the last of her makeup, she looked in the mirror with satisfaction. It was nice to be getting dressed up for something besides church. She paused for a moment to consider whether to wear heels or flats and opted for the dressy black flats.

By the end of Saturday, Jenna and Doug had made a date to go on Tuesday evening to a performance of a community theater group in a nearby town. Doug had suggested it, and Jenna readily agreed, eager to do something cultural. Most of the time she was quite content just staying around the camp in her jeans and casual tops. But she had been part of a couple of college drama productions and she thought it would be fun to see a play.

Earlier in the day, when Dillon had been on his way out of the camp, she had told him that she would be out for the evening with Doug. A strange look had passed over his face. She was not quite sure how to interpret it. Surely it had not been jealousy; as closely as they worked together, he had never given her any reason to think she should not accept dates with someone whose company she enjoyed. Still, she had a hard time putting the pieces together. She knew of Stacie's conversation with Dillon and was almost positive the carved owl left on her doorstep had been from Dillon, but she was not positive enough to ask him openly about it. Besides, for the last few days he had hardly been around at all.

When she had seen him earlier in the day, he had seemed in a hurry and that had made it very easy for her to avoid a conversation of any depth. Surely the gift had been a token of friendship since right after it had appeared Dillon had begun spending a lot of time with Sarah Martyn. *I will ask him about it,* she resolved mentally, *the first chance we get to sit down together alone.*

For now she was resolved to have a pleasant evening with Doug.

He picked her up promptly at six o'clock so that they could make a seven o'clock performance. She was glad to see he had not brought the truck. Looking out the window while she waited for him to come to the door, she inspected the yellow Camaro that he drove. It looked like it was several years old but in good condition.

"You look great," he said when she opened the door.

It was nice to hear someone say that. "Thanks. So do you."

"Are you all set?"

"Just let me grab a sweater."

"Good idea. It'll be cooler later."

A moment later, he opened the car door for her and made sure she was comfortable in the black leather bucket seat on the passenger side. As he walked around the outside of the car, she glanced around the inside. It was impeccably clean, as if he had come straight from a car wash. The tissue box between the seats was full; a dozen cassette tapes were neatly lined up in a special rack under the tape deck.

Doug opened the door and got in.

"I like your car," Jenna said. "How long have you had it?"

"It was new four years ago. But I don't drive it much. I'm

usually in the truck so it has held up well."

"I'd say so."

He started the engine and it purred as he smoothly backed the car up and turned it around. They headed out the gate and were on their way. The clock on the dashboard indicated it was six minutes past six o'clock.

For twenty minutes or so they drove along with intermittent conversation between them. He asked what plays she had performed in during college; she asked how long he had been working for the lumberyard. They agreed that they both liked Mozart, and Doug popped a tape into the deck. As the intricate strains filled the car through the stereo speakers, Jenna was beginning to feel the edge coming off of the awkwardness of a first date. Good music, pleasant company, a play—all the makings of a truly fine evening. She put her head back and closed her eyes, her ears absorbing the minute details of the string concerto.

Suddenly the engine coughed and the car lurched a few yards at a time. Doug managed to steer to the shoulder before the motion ceased.

"Doug?" Jenna looked around outside. They were at least four miles past the last cluster of houses. Out in this rural part of the county there were long stretches of unpopulated roads running alongside the farm fields.

Doug shrugged. "I don't know what happened. I'll get out and check under the hood."

He reached under his seat and pulled out a flashlight. That gave Jenna a fleeting sense of security; he seemed prepared for an emergency.

Doug unlatched the hood and raised it, blocking Jenna's view of his actions. She squirmed down in her seat to look through the narrow opening at the base of the hood, but she could not see much. Doug's hands were moving over various mechanical parts, but he didn't seem to be making any substantial adjustments.

He opened the driver's door and reached under the seat for a rag. Wiping his hands, he said, "The gas is not getting to the engine."

"Fuel pump?" speculated Jenna.

"Could be."

"I'm not much of a mechanic, but this doesn't sound too good," Jenna said. "What should we do?"

"We may just need some gas."

For a fraction of a second, Jenna could not believe what she had heard. "Pardon?"

"My gas gauge has been on the fritz. The needle registers all over the place."

"We're out of gas?" Jenna still could not believe it. Everything else about Doug's car looked so well cared for and tended. How could he bring her out on a remote road like this one if he was not sure he had enough gas to get into town? "Oh, Doug." The disappointment in her voice was obvious.

"It's okay, Jenna," Doug said, "I've got a gas can in the trunk."

Of course. He was so prepared for everything else. At the moment it seemed thoroughly reasonable that he would have a can of gas in the trunk. She sat still, trying not to overreact, while he opened the trunk and extracted the can.

Doug stuck his head back in the car. "Bad news."

"Empty," guessed Jenna.

"Right."

Jenna was genuinely irritated now. In her mind there was no excuse for this. Doug knew that they had to drive forty minutes through the countryside to get to the community theater. How could he possibly have allowed this to happen? Jenna was not accustomed to asking her escorts if their gas tanks were full.

There they were—out on an empty road with little traffic. They had already been stopped for almost twenty minutes and only one car had gone by, and that had been when they had first stopped. It was not the sort of road anyone was likely to stop on to help a stranded vehicle.

"Well, we have to do something," Jenna said after a while. Doug did not seem to be making any move to solve the problem. "I think it's about four miles back to that last intersection."

Doug shook his head. "I think there's something closer in the other direction. I travel this road a lot. There should be a service station about two miles ahead of us."

Jenna silently thought about the options. Two miles compared to four miles. If Doug was right, it would be quicker to get help by proceeding. Maybe they could be on their way within an hour. But if he was wrong, it would be valuable time wasted. The road would only get darker and lonelier. Jenna was not sure she wanted to trust his judgment at this point.

"Maybe we should just leave the hood up and stay here," Doug said. "Isn't that what they say is the safest thing to do?"

Jenna nodded reluctantly. "Well, they do say that. But this is not exactly the interstate."

"A lot of truckers use this route," Doug argued.

Jenna was getting annoyed. "I don't think anyone is going to stop and help us. Besides, it could be a long time before anyone even comes by. There's been only that one car."

Doug reached out and took hold of Jenna's hand. "I know

it looks bleak," he said, "but someone will stop and we'll get them to make a phone call or take me to a gas station. In the meantime, we'll have a chance to talk and get to know each other."

Jenna withdrew her hand from his grasp. She was not in the mood to be patronized. "Look, Doug, if you want to sit here and wait for a miracle, you can. But I'm not going to." She had her hand on the door handle. "I'll walk back and see if I can find a phone."

"I told you it would be better to go ahead," Doug said. He sounded irritated, too.

"I don't know what's up there; I'm sure of what we passed a while ago."

"I just told you what's up there. Don't you trust me?"

Jenna turned her face away and looked out the window. She wanted to scream out, "I trusted you all right, and look where it got me," but she held her tongue.

"I feel strongly that we really shouldn't just sit here and do nothing," she said with forced calm. "And I'm volunteering to do the necessary walking."

"Then I'll come with you. Or I'll go and you stay with the car."

Jenna did not respond. She was not sure which was the worse option—walking along the road in the dark with someone she was angry with or sitting alone in the car.

"You stay here, then." Doug seemed to have reached a decision. "You're not dressed for a two-mile hike anyway. I'll leave the hood up and the emergency flashers on just in case the state patrol comes by."

Jenna was beyond arguing with Doug. At least he was doing something now.

"I'll take the gas can and walk as fast as I can," he said. "It shouldn't take more than half an hour to get to the station, and I'll talk someone into driving me back."

"Fine. I'll wait here."

"I won't be gone more than forty-five minutes."

She nodded silently, but instinctively doubted what he said.

"Do you think I did this on purpose?" Doug pressured her for a response.

Choosing her words carefully, she said, "I never said that."

"But you thought it."

"It does seem to me that it could have been prevented quite easily."

"I'm sorry I'm not as perfect as you are." Doug got out and slammed the car door and started walking down the road, the empty gas can swinging at his side.

❧

Ninety minutes later, Doug was still not back. Jenna did not know what to think. They had both been openly angry when he left; perhaps he was punishing her for getting irritated with him. Or perhaps something had happened to him. Or maybe he had been wrong about how far it was to the service station. Or maybe the station was not open.

Some first date. How quickly it had deteriorated into a first fight. The circumstances were certainly frustrating and romance had unquestionably been nipped in the bud. But what frustrated her most of all was that one of her first attempts to take some action in her own life had been so quickly foiled by circumstances beyond her control. Rather than sitting alone in her cottage wishing Dillon would see her for who she was, she had determined to move on. Rather than trying to compete with Sarah Martyn, Jenna was looking to her own future. And this is what she got for all her effort: almost two hours alone in a car on a dark highway. Four cars had passed by in that time; none of them had even slowed down.

With that evidence, Jenna felt justified in her position that help was not likely to come to her. And she had no explanation for what had happened to Doug, but as the minutes on the clock ticked by, she cared less and less.

She should never have accepted this date. Yes, Doug was friendly enough on his deliveries, and yes, he went to church. So what? What did she really know about him? Besides, he had said he was trying to get back into going to church. In retrospect, it seemed clear that he had only come on that outing with his church so he would have an excuse to be at the camp all day and talk to her.

"I'm such a jerk," Jenna said aloud. "I can't even take control of my own life without making a mess of it. A simple decision about going out on a date was beyond me. How can I ever decide my entire future?"

She waited another fifteen minutes, and Doug still did not return. Jenna was starting to get cold.

This is crazy, she told herself. *I never wanted to wait here in the first place. I'm going to do what I should have done two hours ago.*

But first she rummaged in her purse for a scrap of paper and a pen. Doug had taken the flashlight, so she opened the car door to activate the dome light. Her note was to the point:

> 9:05. *Got worried and went for help in other direction.*
>
> *Jenna*

Thankful for her sweater and her flat shoes, she started the four-mile walk back toward the farmhouses.

ten

The light barraged her bedroom window much too early. Jenna had never been able to sleep late, no matter how badly she wanted to. Her college friends had often joked that if she ever had a night job she would become a walking zombie. She simply could not sleep in daylight. When the sun came up, her body grew restless, turning more frequently and with more agitation. She would crave sleep, but it was always a losing battle. Sometimes putting an extra pillow over her face helped for a few minutes, maybe a half an hour.

But on Wednesday morning, the pillow over her face just made her hot and, after only a few moments, she threw it from the bed. Grudgingly she opened one eye and looked at the alarm clock: three minutes past six. She wished she could sleep till noon. More than that, she wished she could blot out the memory of the previous evening or that she could somehow undo what had happened.

Both eyes were open now and she started kicking off the covers. She was still dressed in the skirt and blouse she had worn the night before. It had been so late when she had finally gotten home, and she was so exhausted that she had fallen into bed at the first opportunity. She sat up on the edge of the bed and started peeling off her clothing. Her stockings were ruined—three runs and a huge hole as a casualty of her nocturnal countryside hike. Her blouse was stained by the sweat she had worked up walking four miles. She pulled it and the skirt off and tossed them into a pile of dirty laundry at the foot of the bed.

Every muscle in Jenna's body ached. The four miles, almost all steeply uphill, had taken her nearly an hour and a half to walk. Every moment of the way she wondered if Doug had made it back to the car. Should she have gone looking for him instead of heading in the other direction? Had he ever come back looking for her? What had happened to him in the first place? What if something horrible had happened to him and she was simply too annoyed with him to care?

With a groan she pulled herself up off the bed and shuffled, stiffly, into the bathroom.

The steamy shower looked inviting even before she stepped into it. She turned her face up into the spray and said aloud, "Oh, Lord, what is going on?" She stood motionless, as if she expected an audible answer. But all she heard was the steady pulsing of the water through the shower head and the sloshing as it bounced off her body.

She stayed there until she detected the temperature of the water declining. Not being interested in a cold shower, she reluctantly shut off the faucet and reached for a towel. The hot water had done its work; she felt a bit more limber and slightly more awake. It was almost six-thirty. The day stretched out ahead of her. Though she would rather have huddled in her bathrobe all day, drinking hot tea and reading a novel, she knew she would have to drag herself out to her work. The animals needed tending and the meadow needed mowing.

Wrapped in a thick, white terrycloth bathrobe that was almost too warm for springtime, she padded into the kitchen and considered her breakfast options. She slicked back her still dripping hair as she pulled open the refrigerator door. Orange juice. Bagels. Bran muffins. Though she was hungry, nothing appealed to her. Finally she picked up the orange juice carton out of the rack in the door and drank directly from it. Almost immediately she felt her blood sugar level rising. The cool liquid refreshed her parched throat. She poured down another long dose before replacing the carton and reaching for a bran muffin and the margarine.

Jenna sat on a stool pushed up against the counter and munched the muffin while rereading a newspaper that was three days old.

This is no life, she thought. Why can't I do a better job than this of putting my life together? Why can't I make at least one choice that seems to be the right one? Jenna shoved the newspaper aside, not caring that half of it fell to the floor. The last of her muffin crumbled between her fingers. Resigned to the mess, she did not even try to catch the crumbs that cluttered her lap. A dab of margarine settled into the white terrycloth, leaving a greasy residue.

She sat that way for a long time, too tired to move into the routine of her day, too discouraged to care about any details around her. The only sound in the room, which Jenna did not even hear, was the steady ticking of the clock over the sink. Jenna had almost completely disconnected herself from her immediate surroundings and had drifted off to a place where the relationships in her life were warm and clear and the choices obvious and rewarding.

At about seven-thirty she came back to reality.

Stepping over the strewn newspaper, she returned to the bedroom, rummaged in her dresser for fresh jeans and a clean shirt, and got dressed. Her wet and tangled hair hung around her face and she set about trying to straighten it out. It would never look right after being allowed to dry that way. Jenna did not care; she just efficiently pulled it back in a ponytail to get it out of the way.

She was nearly finished brushing her teeth when she heard the knock on the back door. That would be Dillon; no one else came to the back door of the cottage. Self-consciously Jenna pinched her cheeks, hoping she looked better than she felt, and answered the knock.

"Good morning," she said with false brightness.

"Good morning, yourself." Dillon studied her expression. "Are you all right?"

"Of course. I'm fine."

"Last night was pretty tough. I didn't expect you up and around so early."

Jenna stepped aside and motioned that Dillon should enter the kitchen. As smoothly as possible, she scooped up the newspapers and set them aside.

"I was just about to make coffee. Want some?" she asked.

Dillon nodded. "Sure. But really I came to see how you are."

"I already told you I'm fine."

Dillon sat on a stool and planted his elbows on the counter. "Jenna, you called at eleven-thirty last night and made that outdoor phone ring until the whole county could hear it."

"I would have called earlier if I could have found a phone sooner. Besides, what took you so long to answer it?" she said, hoping to divert the conversation.

Dillon was shaking his head. "You're not getting away with that. I want to know what happened last night."

Jenna busied herself getting the coffeepot set up. "I already told you what happened."

"You told me that you went out with Doug, had car trouble, he didn't come back, and you wanted to go home. That's not really telling me much."

"That's what happened." Not looking at him, she measured the coffee and dumped it into the filter.

"Well? Did you ever find out what happened to Doug?"

"No." She pushed the start button.

Dillon pressed on. "Don't you think it's strange that by the time we got back to the spot where you left the car, it was gone?"

The coffeepot had started brewing. She had no more excuses not to turn around and face Dillon.

"By the time you got to me at that grocery store, it had been several hours since I had left the car. Doug must have come back."

Dillon seemed unconvinced. "Something's not adding up here."

"Dillon," Jenna said, "it was a horrible night, and I'm just glad you were within earshot of the phone. I don't know who else I could have called, way out here in the boonies."

"Perhaps the police."

"The police? Why would I call the police? They're not a taxi service."

"I suppose you're right," Dillon conceded. "But I don't like this at all."

Jenna sighed. "I wasn't having such a great time, either." She got up and fetched a couple of mugs.

"But why didn't you see Doug on his way back?" Dillon persisted with the inquisition, asking some of the same questions that Jenna had wrestled with unsuccessfully during the night. "You said you were outside the whole time, waiting by that pay phone at the grocery store for me to come for you. If Doug got back to his car and got it going, wouldn't he have passed by before I got there?"

Jenna shrugged. "I don't know, Dillon. You would think he

would have. But maybe we just missed each other somehow."

"Jenna," Dillon began, but then stopped.

"Yes?"

He shook his head. "Nothing. I can't tell you how to live your life."

Jenna thought maybe someone ought to interfere in her life; things could only improve. But she did not know how to answer Dillon. Silently she poured the coffee and sat down again. She had the feeling Dillon had more that he wanted to say. Thankfully he backed off and did not press her for any more explanation of the previous evening.

Outside a familiar set of brakes squealed at the entrance and the hulk of a delivery truck dominated the small parking lot in front of the cottage.

"Sounds like Doug," Dillon said.

Jenna only nodded.

"Guess he made it home all right, too, then."

She nodded again.

Dillon took one last swig of his coffee. "I'd better go see what he has for us today." He set his mug down. "Do you want to come out and talk to him? Find out what happened?"

Jenna shivered involuntarily. "No, I don't think I'm up to that."

"Then you're not as fine as you say, are you?" Dillon's eyes bored into Jenna's. He knew he spoke the truth.

After Dillon left, Jenna took her coffee and went to the living room, where she could sit at one end of the love seat and look out the window without being seen. Though she could not make out what they were saying to each other, she could see Dillon and Doug talking and gesturing.

Suddenly she was desperate to know what they were saying. Would Dillon give Doug the third degree? Would he even let on that he knew anything about last night? If pressed, would Doug answer? She studied their movements. Dillon was pointing up the hill, probably to say that that was where the lumber should be unloaded. Relieved, Jenna sank back into the love seat. Surely they were only talking business.

Her coffee had grown cold. She set the mug aside and leaned her head back. How it ached! The grogginess of three hours ago had subsided somewhat, but not completely.

She heard the engine of Doug's truck rev up as he pulled away and rattled up the hill toward the construction site. A peek out the front window told her that Dillon had gone with him. It was safe for Jenna to venture out. While she had the opportunity, she scrounged up her tennis shoes, grabbed a sweatshirt, and headed out.

Reasoning that Doug would be unloading lumber at the stables, Jenna turned her attention to something other than the horses. She took the rider mower out to the meadow, knowing that it would take her most of the morning to get it cut satisfactorily. But she felt safe away from the cottage, hiding behind the roar of the machine she rode. She could think her own thoughts and stay away from Doug.

For more than an hour, she steered in a pattern that left a trail of long, straight rows behind her. At the end of each row she expertly did a tight U-turn and began the next one. As she glanced over the field, she took satisfaction in the progress she was making. There was a neatness and orderliness that was absent from her personal life. Somehow it was easier to be organized and methodical about her physical work than to practice those same traits in assembling her life. It seemed to Jenna that there ought to be some formula she could follow, some grid she could fill in, some equation she could balance that would make her life come out right.

She heard the answer ringing in her ears: *Find the Lord's Will and obey it.* She had gone to church her whole life; she knew she should be trying to find and do God's Will. But what was that? How could she find it?

Please don't think I'm stupid, Lord, she prayed silently as she drove, *but I need something a little more obvious. You're going to have to hit me over the head with an iron skillet so that I know what voice I should pay attention to.*

When she got back to her cottage for a late lunch, Jenna found a note from Doug taped to the front door. *Sorry about last night,* it said. *Hope we can see each other again soon.*

Jenna crumpled the note in her fist.

eleven

For the rest of the week, every time the phone rang, Jenna jumped. But Doug never called. And on Friday, when she knew he would make another delivery of lumber, she purposely planned to be in town getting groceries to feed the work crew coming on Saturday.

She woke up early on Saturday as usual, this time eager for the day to begin. Dillon had spent weeks organizing a gigantic work party so that the framing for the stable could be built and raised in one day. In a counterpart effort, Jenna had organized a six-member kitchen crew to keep food available on a steady basis all day in the dining hall. Mounds of ingredients sat on the kitchen counters waiting to be transformed into energizing meals for the nearly forty people who would work on the stables. If they finished the framing, they would proceed with the outer walls and work until the light failed them.

It was an exciting day, and Jenna was ready to jump in with both feet. By seven o'clock in the morning she was in the dining hall kitchen sorting out the sacks she had left there the night before: potatoes, bread, pastas, pop, chips, doughnuts, canned vegetables. In the refrigerator she had stored lunch meats, ground beef, sliced ham, and fresh fruits and vegetables.

She and Dillon had it all planned. The workers would eat in shifts; the work would continue in an unbroken pattern all day. A generator would be running to provide electricity at the work site, so Jenna could set up an industrial-sized coffeepot, along with a canister of cold punch. There would be no opportunity for momentum to lag. Dillon was optimistic about the progress they could make in one day if everyone stuck to the task.

She heard a car pull up and poked her head out the back door of the kitchen to see who had arrived so early. She waved vigorously as she recognized Brad's van and saw that Stacie was with him.

"I didn't know you were coming," she said, giving Stacie a quick hug a moment later. "I'm so glad to see you."

"Brad didn't want me to come," Stacie said, glancing over her shoulder at her husband. "He wanted me to stay in town, near the hospital. But I didn't want to miss this day. Besides, I haven't talked to you all week."

"Well, I'm glad you're here, but you have to be a good girl and take it easy today. The last time you were here you gave me the scare of my life."

Stacie grinned. "Sorry about that. But I assure you, I haven't felt a twinge all day."

"What do you mean, 'all day?' It's only seven o'clock in the morning." Jenna opened the screen door and let Stacie go ahead of her into the camp kitchen.

"I promise that if I feel anything at all, I'll have Brad take me home."

"You'd better! Nevertheless, I'm going to get you a chair and I expect you to sit in it."

"I won't argue with you today. It's too fine a day for that." Stacie smiled up at Jenna, who opened a folding chair and set it solidly in front of Stacie. "You seem pretty excited." Stacie obediently sat down.

"I have to admit, I am. I've gotten used to the dilapidated

condition of the stable, but it'll be so nice to have a new building, something roomier and easier to keep clean." She went back to reorganizing the groceries, trying to separate the things they would need early in the day from the dinner time supplies.

"How's Dillon doing today?" Stacie asked.

"I haven't seen him yet. I suppose he's up at the site."

Stacie was already restless in her chair. "Are you sure there isn't something I can do?"

Jenna scanned the pile on the counter. "Here, scoot up to the work table," she said. "You can unwrap these pastries and put them on trays."

"Sounds yummy."

"We're hoping we can bribe everyone with an early morning treat."

Stacie began methodically pulling plastic wrap off the bundles of doughnuts. "So what have you been up to this week?"

It was an innocent question, Jenna knew. But how much did she want to say at this point? She decided to confide.

"I went on a date," she said simply.

Stacie's eyes lit up. "Did Dillon finally ask you out?"

Jenna shook her head. "Not Dillon. Doug."

"Doug? The guy from the lumberyard?"

Jenna dropped into a chair beside her friend. "Stacie, it was a disaster. We were going to see a play at the community theater, but he ran out of gas, and we got stranded, and he went looking for gas while I waited, but he didn't come back for a long time, so I decided not to wait any longer—"

"Whoa!" said Stacie with her hands up. "Go back a few steps. You ran out of gas? Way out here in the country?"

Jenna nodded. "It was really strange. Everything else about

him was meticulous. He looked great. The car looked great. He let me choose the play."

"Ran out of gas?" Stacie could still not believe it.

"I know; it's unreal. Nobody that lives this far out lets their gas tank get anywhere near empty." Jenna's eyes began to fill with tears as she allowed herself the emotional release she had denied for four days. "Then we squabbled about what to do. I'm afraid I lost my cool and let my irritation get the best of me. He stomped off in the direction he wanted to go and didn't come back for hours."

"He just left you sitting there?"

"I could have gone with him if I had wanted to. But something told me not to do it, so I stayed in the car with the doors locked."

"What do you mean, something told you not to?" Stacie pressed.

Jenna could only shrug. "At first I thought it would be nice to have an evening out. But after we got stuck, I started feeling funny about it. I just thought I would be better off on my own."

"So how did you get home?"

"I hiked about four miles to an intersection where there were some old houses and a grocery store. I don't think the store is even in business anymore, but miraculously the phone outside was working. Anyway, I dialed the camp number and thankfully Dillon heard the bell and answered."

Stacie sank back awkwardly in the metal chair. "What did Dillon say about all this?"

"Not much," Jenna said, "which was a relief. He just came and got me." Jenna got up and started fidgeting with the groceries again, behind Stacie's back. "He started to give me the third degree the next morning, but he backed off."

Stacie twisted around so she could look at Jenna. "Are you all right? Really?"

Jenna nodded. "Nothing happened. I got home safely."

The back door burst open, and Dillon literally bounded into the room. "You guys ready for the big day?" His own excitement was obvious.

Stacie smiled at him. "My job is to sit still and behave myself."

Jenna playfully whacked Stacie's shoulder with a dish towel. "I'm ready!" she said. "The kitchen crew should be here soon, and we'll get things rolling."

Dillon picked at a doughnut and Stacie slapped his fingers.

"I've got the lumber all laid out." Dillon looked at his watch. "Where is everybody? Didn't I say first thing in the morning?"

Stacie was amused at his boyishness. "They'll be here. To be more precise, you said eight o'clock."

He scrunched up his face. "Should have said six o'clock. No sense in wasting daylight."

He made another attempt to break off a piece of a glazed doughnut. This time Stacie did not stop him.

"How about the coffeepot?" he asked. "Is it ready?"

Jenna slid the huge pot out of its corner and toward the sink. "I was just about to fill it."

"Great. We can load it in the back of my truck and take it up to the site."

Jenna filled the pot and measured enough coffee for 100 cups. Then she turned her attention to mixing punch.

"Need some help with that?" Brad stuck his head in the doorway at just the right moment.

Between them, Brad and Dillon dragged the pot to the doorway and then heaved it up onto the back of the truck. Several cars had arrived, and volunteers emerged. Brad directed everyone up the hill and led the way. Men of all ages and some isolated women, all with toolboxes in tow, straggled up the hill to the stables. Several other women descended on the camp kitchen to assess their resources for the day's work.

Dillon turned to Stacie and Jenna. "Why don't you guys come up to the site for a few minutes? I've got a great pep talk planned."

Jenna and Stacie smiled at each other. "Wouldn't miss it," Jenna said.

"You can ride up with me," he said. "Hop in the front of the truck."

"That's a joke, right?" Stacie asked.

"Oops. Sorry. Guess hopping is not really in your repertoire these days."

Jenna quickly entered the truck and slid over to the middle of the seat. Carefully, she balanced a tray of doughnuts on her lap. Dillon offered his arm and patiently helped Stacie into the cab.

"No fancy driving, now," Stacie warned as she stretched out one arm to brace herself against the dashboard. The ride would undoubtedly be bumpy.

Dillon playfully honked his horn at the workers walking to the site. "Out of my way," he said so that only Stacie and Jenna could hear him. "I got a pregnant woman here."

The trucks's cab was not very big. With three people in the seat they were shoulder to shoulder. Jenna felt Dillon's muscles rippling as he turned the steering wheel. He glanced at her and she returned the look. Even though he matched her gaze for only a fraction of a second, his gray eyes seemed to look deeply into her. When he turned back to the road ahead of them, she let her attention linger on his profile. A warmth of emotion bubbled up from her stomach into her throat.

Abruptly the tall, chic image of Sarah Martyn filled her mind and the moment was gone. She shook her head almost imperceptibly to release herself from the vision of Sarah.

They reached the work site and joined the crowd gathering around. Nearly everyone was there—close to forty people. Dillon jumped up on the fence and balanced himself where everyone could see him.

"Welcome, and good morning!" he said loudly and clearly. "I want to thank all of you for coming out so early in the day and for committing your whole day to this project. I'm optimistic about what we can accomplish if we all work together.

"Let's talk about the important things first—food." Dillon pointed at Jenna. "Jenna McLean has organized a kitchen crew that will keep the food coming all day, starting with doughnuts and coffee. I want to take this opportunity to thank the kitchen crew in advance for their efforts. And I want to publicly thank Jenna for the vital contribution she has made during the last two years to the refurbishing projects around the Homestead. We've come a long way, and a lot of the credit goes to Jenna."

Jenna felt her face warming as she saw dozens of people turn and look at her; a round of applause broke out, instigated by Dillon. She knew Dillon's words were sincere but she never wanted this kind of recognition from him. How was it that he could stand up on a fence in front of all these people and say such flattering things, yet he did not understand her at all? Why was he assuming she would leave the camp at the end of the summer—almost forcing her into it? Couldn't he understand why she had poured herself into this place for the last two years? Did he really think it was just a temporary student job to her?

Stacie seemed to sense the unrest stirring in Jenna, and she nudged Jenna's elbow. "It's okay," Stacie whispered. "I'll keep working on him."

Dillon's speech digressed into instructions for the construction work. Gradually, Jenna and Stacie stepped back to get out of the way and started making their way over the hill once again.

"Now why do you suppose he did that?" Jenna asked, when they were far enough from the group that they could speak freely.

"It's obvious he wants to make sure you get the credit you deserve for what you do around here."

Jenna kicked a rock. "I don't care about any credit."

"What do you want?" Stacie asked gently.

Jenna, with tears in her eyes, turned to face her friend. "I want to stop feeling the way I do about Dillon." She threw her hands up in a gesture of resignation. "It's obvious he doesn't think of me the same way."

"But you haven't even talked to him about how you feel," countered Stacie.

"There wouldn't be any point. I'd just pitifully embarrass myself and have to disappear from the face of the earth."

"I could talk to Dillon again," Stacie offered.

Jenna adamantly shook her head. "No. I don't want to trick him into anything. If it's not what he wants. . . ." She swallowed hard to regain her composure. They were approaching the dining hall. "We've got a lot of work ahead of us today. Let's get to it."

twelve

Jenna could hardly believe it was lunch time already. The morning had flown by as she had scurried back and forth between the dining hall and the stable, hardly stopping to catch her breath between errands. The workers were going through more coffee and punch than she had anticipated. On her last trip up the hill she had seen dozens of paper cups strewn around. With a twinge of environmental guilt, she tried to pick up some of them. It was obvious that the workers were too intent on their work to care about conserving paper cups; they simply needed their thirst quenched quickly so they could stay at their tasks.

She had done her best to have the kitchen schedule organized ahead of time, but there were always miscellaneous questions or changes in plans. Several of the volunteers had set aside her plans for ideas of their own, creating some last-minute confusion. Now, whether she was ready or not, it was eleven-thirty. Standing outside the dining hall, she could see the first shift of workers coming over the hill in search of their midday meal.

Jenna pulled open the screen door to the kitchen and stuck her head in.

"Here they come," she warned. "Are we ready?"

Terry, the head cook, paused just long enough to get a good grip on the oversized bowl of pasta salad she carried. "Ready as we'll ever be," Terry said. "Everything else is already out."

Jenna followed Terry through the kitchen and into the

dining room, where she saw Stacie setting the last of the tables. Stacie looked up and gave her a mischievous grin.

"You caught me," Stacie said. "I figured lifting silverware was allowed."

Jenna shook her finger at her friend. "Well, okay, but if I catch you clearing tables later, you're in big trouble."

"I promise." Stacie started waddling back to the kitchen, her hands resting on the ridge created by her swollen midsection. From behind, it seemed to Jenna that Stacie was having a hard time moving. She just had to trust that Stacie was feeling all right.

The main doors of the dining hall swung open and the room immediately erupted with chatter and laughter. The first twenty workers crashed into the room, their faces smudged, their shirts sweaty.

"Where do we clean up?" one of the men called out.

Jenna turned and looked at them, her face blanching. She had not even thought about this! "Uh, well. . .I suppose. . . ."

They were already pressing through the door to the kitchen in search of running water. The indignant kitchen crew tried to shoo them out of the sacred territory but to no avail. Two at a time, the workers stood at the double sink, scrubbing their hands and splashing water on their faces. While they waited, others offered their unsolicited opinions on the menu. Most of them were still dripping when they stepped away from the sink and returned to the dining room to get in the food line, hungry enough to eat whatever was out there.

With that minor crisis behind them, the rest of the lunch service went according to Jenna's plan. The construction volunteers ate loudly and heartily, heaping their plates with thick sandwiches, baked beans, pasta salad, potato salad, and fresh fruit. They quenched their thirst with can after can of cold pop. Most of them stayed only long enough to swallow their food and then headed straight back up the hill to the project. Some of them grabbed the nearest silverware and never even bothered to sit down. Their laughter and camaraderie echoed off the wooden rafters of the building, giving Jenna a heightened exhilaration for the day.

Within twenty minutes, the first shift had come and gone.

Jenna, Terry, and Stacie tentatively stepped out of the kitchen to survey the damage in the dining room, convinced that a whirlwind had struck.

"Whew," Terry said, "I'm glad that's over!"

Jenna, laughing, turned to look at her. "What do you mean, over? We have to do it again in another half an hour. . .and then again at supper time."

"We'd better replenish the food, then, and try to straighten up these tables a little," Terry said as she moved to the serving table and picked up two empty bowls.

"Will we have enough food for the next bunch?" Stacie asked.

Jenna felt a twinge of panic as she waited for the answer.

Terry looked at what was left on the table. "Fortunately, I didn't put everything out. If I had, they would no doubt have eaten it all already."

In a moment, some of the others in the kitchen came out to help clean things up. Thirty minutes later, they were ready. When the second wave came through, Jenna was alert and waved her hand toward the kitchen and said, "You can clean up in there."

After lunch, and a well-deserved break for themselves, the kitchen crew threw themselves into preparation of dinner. They chopped onions and herbs for the spaghetti sauce, spread butter and garlic on the french bread, mixed enormous green salads, all the while chatting about their husbands and children. During all this, Jenna kept updating her mental list of things to double-check, but as the day went on she relaxed gradually, satisfied that everything was going well. There would be no major disasters.

Late in the afternoon, needing a breather before the dinner rush, Jenna stepped outside hoping to get some air and a few moments of quiet. Stacie, having been banished from the kitchen for her unflagging persistence in doing chores she had been instructed to avoid, was sitting in a lawn chair under a tree with a magazine in her lap. Jenna walked over to her.

"Are you comfortable there?" Jenna asked. "You're welcome to go in the cottage and put your feet up if you'd like."

Stacie shook her head. "It's too nice a day to be inside." She looked up at Jenna and smiled. "I'll bet you'll be glad when this day is finished."

Jenna reluctantly nodded. "It's gone well, for the most part, and it's been exciting to see the progress on the stable, but I'm getting tired already. I suppose everyone is."

Stacie gestured to the empty chair next to her. "Sit for a while. I won't even talk to you. Just rest."

Jenna obliged without objection. She settled into the lawn chair, propped her elbows on its scratchy arms, and closed her eyes. For a few moments she was able to block out the distant hammering echoing over the hill and concentrate on the little sounds around her: the leaves rustling as birds flitted through the branches above her; the crickets chirping faintly. The breeze blew pleasantly across her face and she felt some of the day's tension easing out of her body. When the sound of an engine obliterated the sounds of nature, she forced herself to sit very still until the car had passed. This was one mood she did not want to break.

"Jenna?" Stacie said softly.

"Hmmm?" Jenna was reluctant to move or open her eyes.

"I know I said I wouldn't talk, but did you see who that was that just went by?"

Jenna shook her head.

"I'm pretty sure it was Doug."

Now Jenna's eyes opened wide. "Doug? Doug is here today?"

Stacie nodded. "A yellow Camaro? Is that what he drives?"

"When he remembers to put gas in it," Jenna answered dourly. "Then he's here."

Jenna pressed her lips together thoughtfully. "Well, you know what? That's all right. That's good. I'm not going to go looking for him, but if I see him I have a few things I'd like to say."

"Jenna!" A voice from the kitchen door screeched. "We need you!"

Jenna sighed and Stacie gave her a sympathetic look. With great reticence, Jenna pulled herself out of her chair and went to see why her presence was required.

❧

Supper was more leisurely than lunch had been. The tables were set for all of the volunteer laborers to eat together and more of them lingered over their meals and the homemade pie that followed. As Jenna buzzed around the kitchen and dining room with miscellaneous last-minute tasks, she heard snippets of enthusiastic conversations about the day's project. It seemed unanimous that they had accomplished more than they had expected to.

Jenna looked around the dining room at the exhausted workers, their clothing soiled, their hair bedraggled, their posture slouched. Many of them were using the mealtime as a recovery period before heading home. A few faithful souls were staying a couple more hours till the light would give out completely.

At last her eyes settled on Dillon. He had hardly touched his dinner, and she knew that he had never come down off the hill for lunch, either. He ought to be famished, but if he was, he did not show it. Instead, his eyes glimmered with pleasure, and when he laughed at the humor spouting around him, his voice lifted above the echoing din and seemed to hang in the air. Jenna watched as he tilted his dark blond head back and grinned at nothing in particular. There had been plenty of work parties at the camp during the last three years, but this was the first major new construction project. Obviously Dillon was delighted at the turnout and perseverance of the group. Jenna caught herself standing still long enough to smile and share his pleasure.

The meal over, people trickled out of the dining hall, some to their cars, others to the work site. The kitchen crew had already moved into a final cleanup mode. The huge pot that had held the spaghetti sauce as it had simmered all afternoon, was soaking. Two women furiously scrubbed plates and silverware. Others packaged up the leftovers so they could be taken home and used by someone.

Once the dining room had cleared, Jenna took refuge from the kitchen chaos by moving from table to table, setting the chairs upside down on them. Then she slowly and methodically pushed a broom from one end of the room to the other, back and forth, back and forth. Since her brief respite in the afternoon had been interrupted, she was now glad for the time to be working alone. Periodically she glanced over at the spot where Dillon had sat and where his presence remained. The image of his delight was fixed in her mind. She loved seeing him so happy.

She could hear that things were winding down in the kitchen. When she went through the door, it was clear that the work was done.

"Thanks, everybody," she said, moving her eyes first to Terry and then around the room. "You did a wonderful job. Don't know what I would have done without you."

Terry waved away the acknowledgment. "Aw, you did all the planning. That's the tough part."

Someone handed her a cup of coffee. "You look like you could use this."

Jenna smiled gratefully and nodded.

"If you don't mind," Terry said, "some of us are just going to get off our feet and wait here for our husbands."

"Of course. That's no problem." She glanced out the window. "It's getting dark. I would think they would be through before much longer. Maybe I'll just wander up there and see how things are coming."

In welcome solitude, she climbed the hill. The light was going fast now. As she reached the peak and could see the work area, she saw the silhouetted forms of about five men, Dillon among them, still nailing on one outside wall. She had not been up to the site since before lunch. Her jaw nearly dropped open at the progress she now viewed.

"Jenna?"

She jumped at the voice behind her and wheeled around.

"Doug," she said simply. He seemed to have stepped out of nowhere. She took a deep breath, hoping her heart would stop beating so fast.

"I wanted to say I'm sorry about the other night," he said, not seeming to notice that he had startled her. "It was stupid of me not to fill the tank before we started out."

Jenna was not about to dispute that point. She went straight to her real questions. "Where were you all that time, Doug? I waited more than two hours for you."

"The gas station was closed when I got there."

"But it was still early," she argued.

"What can I say? It was closed. I had to go another couple of miles to find gas."

Jenna was not sure she believed him. His demeanor was too nonchalant. "I didn't see you come back by in the other direction."

"I didn't. Since you were gone I just went on home. . .the same direction I had gone before."

"But I got help and came back looking for you."

"Look, Jenna, I'm sorry it all happened." Clearly he was not going to answer any more questions. "Can't we just put that behind us and start fresh? We could go out to dinner next weekend."

Jenna looked away from Doug. A voice in her head told her to choose her words carefully. "I don't think that would be a good idea, Doug."

She saw the disappointment in his face but pressed on, keeping her voice gentle and low. "I'm afraid I agreed to go out with you for the wrong reasons. I was just trying to prove a point to myself, and I shouldn't have involved you. This is not really a good time for me to get involved with anyone."

His disappointment quickly transformed into irritation. "Yeah. I've heard that brushoff before."

Jenna held her ground. "I'm sorry, Doug, I really am. But I don't think this would work out. I'm too mixed up. I don't want to string you along when I don't share your feelings."

His stare burned into her eyes for an excruciating moment

before he turned and walked—almost marched—to his nearby car. Jenna stood on the hill and watched, trembling. She did not see another figure move up behind her in the dark.

"Everything okay?"

Jenna pivoted to see Dillon. She found she could not speak, so she simply nodded.

Dillon touched her elbow gently. "Come on. I'll walk you down to the cottage."

thirteen

Jenna's pleasure in the day was shattered by the encounter with Doug. He revved his engine and tore down the camp road much too fast, never looking back at Jenna. Her eyes were fixed on the tail lights until they were out of sight and the sound of the engine diminished into the country air.

And now this attention from Dillon confused her. She was genuinely glad he had turned up when he did. And she was grateful for his offer to walk her home. She just was not sure she was ready to respond to the questions she knew were in his mind.

She took a few tentative steps at Dillon's side, his hand still on her elbow. "Are you finished?" she asked, looking back over her shoulder. Two workers still lingered, tapping a few nails. "They don't need me," Dillon said, squeezing her elbow. "You do."

Tears sprang to her eyes, not because of the trauma of her conversation with Doug but because of the softness in Dillon's voice. She couldn't form words to express her thoughts at that moment. She looked away, not wanting him to see her reaction.

They walked down the hill in silence. She could think of only one other occasion when they had walked around the camp together in the evening: when she had first moved into the cottage and they had divided up the routine chores. She had often walked alone, passing by his cabin with the cast of yellow light emanating from the small windows. Often she had wished he would pop his head out as she passed, perhaps even join her on the rest of the loop. But the most that ever happened was that he waved to her through the window.

His hand moved up her back and came to a rest on her shoulder. "Are you sure you're all right?"

She swallowed hard. "I guess I am a little rattled."

"What happened? I saw Doug talking to you and headed up there, but by the time I got there he was zooming off."

Jenna shrugged one shoulder. "He wanted to go out again. I told him I didn't think that was a good idea, and he got mad."

Dillon blew out his breath. "Well, nobody ever likes rejection. Let's hope he cools off a little on the way home."

Suddenly the words tumbled out of Jenna. "I thought I liked him. He seemed like a nice guy. But the other night I felt really weird about what happened. On the surface it might look like I'm overreacting. So what if he ran out of gas? It could happen to anybody. But everything about that night was so strange."

Dillon nodded his understanding.

Jenna continued. "Besides, I just went out with him because he asked me, not because I have any real interest in a relationship with him. I did enough of that kind of dating in college. I'm not interested in doing that anymore."

They had reached her back door. Dillon was smiling slightly. "It's good to hear you finally talking about whatever's been building up inside you lately."

She looked at him, surprised. What had he noticed? They really had not even seen very much of each other in recent days. He'd been so busy with the building project—and with

Sarah Martyn.

Jenna busied herself with fishing her keys out of her pocket.

Dillon put a hand on her forearm to stop her agitation. "Jenna, do you think we could talk for a while?"

Her heart quickened and she swallowed hard again. "Talk? Sure," she answered, nervously. "Uh, I could make some coffee or something."

"That would be great."

She unlocked the back door and they stepped into her kitchen. She wished she had cleaned up a little more before she had left in the morning. As adroitly as she could, she moved two days' worth of dishes off the table and into the sink where they were not so visible. She gestured that Dillon should sit on one of the stools.

"This will just take a minute," she said, pouring out some cold coffee and rinsing out the pot.

"You don't really have to make coffee," he said. "Maybe you'd just like to sit down, too."

"No, this is fine," she insisted. She felt an urgent need to stay busy. "Things went well today, don't you think?" she said lightly.

Dillon took the cue. "Yes! We got a tremendous amount of work done. We'll have the new stable up in no time, at this rate."

Jenna rattled the dishes in the sink to find a dish rag and started wiping off the counters. "Sorry about the mess."

Dillon graciously ignored her apology. "The food was great. Thanks for everything you did today, Jenna."

She smiled at him. "You're welcome. I'm not much good with a hammer, but I was glad to have a part in the project."

"You have a part in a lot of things."

"Just trying to earn my keep around here."

Dillon shifted his weight on the stool to face her squarely. "Stacie tells me you're thinking about leaving."

Was this what he wanted to talk about? Jenna heard the clock ticking as she thought about her answer. "You asked if I would stay the summer, and I will."

"And after that?"

She shrugged. "I'm not sure yet. I'm still considering my options. Maybe Ohio. Maybe graduate school." She glanced at Dillon, who looked thoughtful and unsure.

"Jenna," he said in a low voice, "can I be frank with you?"

With a beginning like that, Jenna just knew that whatever he had to say would be bad news. "Of course." The coffee was done. She reached for the pot and filled the mugs. She handed him one and then leaned back against the counter, still standing.

"Why don't you sit down?" Dillon asked. "You seem. . .I don't know. . .not yourself."

Wordlessly she sat down and tried to keep still. Inside her skin she felt the surging of insistent, restrained energy.

"I'd like to put things on the table between us," Dillon began. "Stacie talked with me a couple of weeks ago, and then again today. I'm afraid I've done some things to hurt you when I never meant to."

Now that this conversation had finally arrived, Jenna was not sure she could cope with it. "Oh, Dillon, no. . .it's—"

He put a hand up to stop her. "Let me talk. First of all, I want you to know how genuinely I appreciate the contribution you've made at the Homestead. I was not exaggerating when I said this morning that we could not have come this far without you. I hope you believe that."

She nodded, her thoughts spinning.

"And secondly, I don't want to have Stacie coming to me to tell me how you're feeling about things."

"Me neither!" Jenna interjected. She could not hold her tongue any longer. "Please don't think that I put her up to that."

He was shaking his head. "No, I know you wouldn't do that. And I don't want to give you the wrong impression about what she's done, either. She hasn't meant to break any confidences between the two of you. She's just encouraged me to talk to you. . .and I started putting the pieces together from that."

What pieces? What conclusions had he drawn? Her mind wanted to scream out half a dozen questions, but she sat perfectly still and waited for him to continue.

"So I thought maybe we could just talk to each other. Honestly. About our feelings for each other."

She could not believe what she was hearing. When he paused, she was unsure whether she was supposed to take over the conversation. Was he asking her to reveal her feelings outright? Was she ready to do that?

To her relief, he continued, giving her a few more minutes to collect herself. "Jenna, I really care about you. Apparently I haven't done a very good job of expressing that. It's easy for me to get obsessed with a project and not relate to people very well. I'm sorry if I've confused you lately."

Oh, no, here it comes, she thought, *the we're-good-friends, let's-stay-that-way speech.* She braced herself. Visions of Sarah Martyn filled her mind, her tall gracefulness and flawless complexion, the mysterious darkness in her eyes. Jenna forced herself to focus her attention on what Dillon was saying.

"I know it seems like I take you for granted, but I don't," Dillon said. "People seem to respond so well to you—that's a key part of a successful camp. I hope you'll consider staying around."

She hardly knew what to say. "Stay around?" she echoed weakly.

He nodded. "Will you stay?"

Jenna got up and added her empty mug to the pile in the kitchen sink. "I. . .I don't know."

Dillon stood up and came close to her. "I'm not doing this right."

"No, it's fine. I'll think about it and try to let you know—"

He broke in before she could finish her sentence. "No, that's not what I mean. I really want you to stay, not just for the camp."

She looked at him, wordless. What was he getting at?

Gently he took hold of her arms and turned her around to face him. "Let me try another tack." He bent forward and kissed her softly on the mouth.

Her head spun. Could this really be happening?

When he drew back, she murmured, "But. . . ." Breathlessness kept her from saying more.

"But what?" Dillon asked quietly, a smile on his lips and his face still close to hers.

"I don't understand. I thought you and Sarah—"

"Sarah?" Dillon tilted his head back and laughed. "I guess things have looked a little suspicious."

"Then you're not. . .?"

He shook his head emphatically. "I told you Sarah is an old friend who is looking for a change. That's all."

Jenna blushed with the embarrassment of her erroneous

conclusion. "You seemed so close."

Dillon's face lost its smile as a serious expression moved over it. "Let me tell you a bit more about Sarah," he said, stroking her forearms. "She married my best friend in college. I stood up at their wedding. Brian died a few months ago in an auto accident."

Jenna put her fingertips to her mouth. "Oh, I'm so sorry."

Dillon continued. "Sarah was four months pregnant, but the stress made her lose the baby. She's had such a rough time. When she called me, I just couldn't turn her down. And then this job thing came up, and I thought it might be just the change she needed."

Jenna sighed. "I'm so sorry for Sarah. Do you think she'll take the job?"

He nodded. "I'm pretty sure she will. It's a little hard for her to be around Stacie, because of the baby. . . ."

"Oh, of course."

"But she's working on that." He paused and his lips stretched out in a smile once again. "Does that clear things up?"

Jenna laughed nervously and nodded. "Thanks."

"I hope this helps to clear things up, too." He leaned in and kissed her again. When he pulled back, he looked deeply into her eyes and stroked her cheek with the back of his hand. "It's been a long day. You're tired. I'd better go."

"Thanks, Dillon. . .for everything."

"I'll see you tomorrow. We'll talk some more."

She nodded, the lump in her throat growing too big to talk.

He left then, quickly and quietly. She stood in the kitchen for a few moments with her eyes closed, wondering if she had fallen asleep on her feet and dreamed it all or if it was true.

Just when she had given up on Dillon and had come to accept that he did not return her feelings, he had completely surprised her. As exhausted as she was, she knew it would be a long time before she fell asleep that night.

Suddenly she felt the accumulated grime of the day. Her shirt was splattered with food stains and her jeans were caked in dust. Her hair straggled around her face, uncombed in the last fourteen hours. This was hardly the romantic circumstances under which she had imagined that Dillon might kiss her. It was supposed to be out under the stars one evening, or after an intimate Italian dinner, or anywhere but in a cluttered kitchen, dressed this way.

She laughed aloud and shook her head. It was no dream; it had really happened, even under these odd circumstances. She turned around and surveyed the heap in the sink. Well, if she wasn't going to sleep, she might as well attack it now.

The first task was to bring some order to the mess in the sink. One by one she removed the dishes and stacked them neatly to the left of the sink. As the water ran to fill the basin, she gathered up the trail of coffee mugs that she had left around the kitchen for the last two days and added them to the stack. She added soap to the water and plunged her arms in up to the elbows.

When the dishes were done, she wiped down all the counters, swept the floor thoroughly, and scrubbed the faucet till it twinkled. The room had been transformed. If she had to be kissed in a kitchen, it should at least be a clean one. She would be more prepared the next time.

With the kitchen once again still and quiet, Jenna's ears were more alert to the sounds outside the cottage. She was sure she heard the gravel out in front crunching under someone's feet. Cautiously she moved into the living room to look out the window. She could see nothing out of the ordinary, but she was sure someone had been out there.

It was then that she remembered the last time she had had this feeling—the day she had found the carved owl outside her door. *Dillon*. Smiling broadly now, she pulled open the front door and picked up a bouquet of red roses.

fourteen

The next day it rained most of the afternoon. Jenna had already been into St. Mary's for church in the morning and now she was headed back into town for a late-afternoon baby shower for Stacie. The women's group from the church had organized it and, so far, it was a surprise to Stacie.

The windshield wipers swished and thumped rhythmically across the glass, but their effort was inadequate. With each pass they left a blur directly in Jenna's line of vision. She wished she were two inches taller as she stretched her neck to look through a clear spot.

Perspiring in a silk blouse, she cracked open her window in hope of finding a pocket of fresh air. But the humidity inside the car was only intensified with the outside air. It was an odd day—spring rain mixed with early summer temperatures; no vibrant thundershower, no spectacular show of lightning. Just steady rain soaking into the earth, deepening the variegated greens along the roadway.

How fortunate it was that this had not happened yesterday during the construction work. All their weeks of planning would have slid down the hill with the mud. As it was, the rain was welcome today.

As she pulled into the church parking lot, Jenna glanced at her watch. She was late, despite having allowed plenty of time for the trip back to town. The rain had slowed her down more than she had realized. Despite the weather, the number of cars in the parking lot testified to a good turnout for the shower. Jenna was glad. Stacie deserved all the attention she was going to get this afternoon.

With her package under her arm, Jenna bent her head against the rain and ran from the car to the door of the building. In the fellowship hall, she stopped briefly to wipe moisture from her forehead before adding her gift to the stack, which was already teetering precariously in several places. She looked around. Festive pink and blue balloons, gathered in generous bouquets, were tied to chairs and taped to walls all around the room. Some had broken free and now floated whimsically above intermittent conversations. Ribbons of matching crepe paper looped down from the ceiling at regular intervals. Packages of assorted shapes and sizes competed for space on and below the designated gift table. Next to the table stood a wooden rocking chair with a padded seat—the place of honor for the mother-to-be. An enormous cake, elaborately decorated in pink and white, sat invitingly on the serving table and next to a sparkling punch bowl. It was all Jenna could do to keep from running her finger through a ripple of butter cream frosting.

Jenna, looking for Stacie, scanned the crowd of about forty women. She did not see her.

"Oh, Jenna, you made it." She turned to see Donna looking a little ragged around the edges. "I was afraid you wouldn't drive all the way back in."

"I wouldn't miss it. Everything looks great," Jenna said brightly. "Where's the guest of honor?"

Donna smiled mischievously. "Should be here any minute, if Brad is doing his job."

Jenna gave a playful snort. "You trusted Brad with a job like this?"

Just then the lights went out. "Shhh," someone hissed

insistently. "They just pulled up to the door. Everyone quiet."

In a few minutes, Jenna heard Stacie's voice in the hallway outside.

"What did you say this meeting was for?" she was saying, obviously confused. "There are a lot of cars out there for a committee meeting. Are you sure there's not a wedding or something?"

"Surprise!" On Donna's cue the lights went on and the shout rose up.

Stacie stood with her hand still on the door, clearly shocked. She turned and looked at Brad. "You rat!" she said happily.

"See ya later, honey," he said. He kissed her and was gone.

Jenna watched with pleasure as Stacie was greeted and escorted to her seat. She followed her friend's movement across the room, hoping to catch her eye, but Stacie was surrounded by others offering their congratulations and laughing at their own success in surprising her. Jenna did not mind. This particular baby shower was one she would like to have helped plan. But she'd had enough foresight not to commit herself to throwing a party on the same weekend as the stable project. So now she was content just to sit on the sidelines and watch the delight of the other women.

She took a seat at the far end of the oblong arrangement of metal folding chairs, where she would have a good view of Stacie. From this vantage point she could also see a group of junior high girls making hasty last-minute preparations for the program they would present. Jenna recognized them as girls who had been in the Sunday school class Stacie had taught on and off for the last couple of years. Stacie had taken over the class after her good friend, Megan, married and moved away. Now the the girls nervously arranged themselves in a not-quite-straight row and started a cassette tape. Their treble voices wavered on the high notes, but they kept up admirably and blushed at the applause that followed. A younger child stood up and haltingly read a poem about mothers and babies before presenting a plaque to Stacie.

It was all very touching. But then, just about anything would have been touching to Jenna that day. Her encounter with Dillon the night before had left an optimism in her spirit. Holding his hand as they had ridden in to church together that morning had heightened her feelings. So, at the moment, anything would seem sweet to Jenna.

The ceremonial gift opening began. In between snippets of conversation with women around her, Jenna expressed appropriate admiration for the tiny outfits and furry toys emerging from the packages. As the gifts were passed around the circle, she marveled at the delicacy and detail of even the tiniest pieces of clothing. This child would be well dressed, there was no doubt about that. And then Jenna saw Stacie reach for the package she had brought and waited, a smile on her lips. A general "Ah" rippled through the group as Stacie pulled out a mobile of teddy bears hanging from balloons. When Jenna had seen the mobile in a craft store, she had known immediately that it was a perfect match for Stacie's decorating scheme. Jenna kept her eyes fixed on Stacie as her friend scanned the group looking for her. Finally their eyes met and Stacie smiled her thanks.

The ritual was repeated nearly a dozen more times before the pile of packages on the table had been transformed to a mound of gifts and cards on the floor around Stacie's chair. With the last gift open, someone cut the cake and the food line began.

Jenna intentionally lingered toward the end of the line, waiting for Stacie, who was served first, to come through with her glass party tray.

"Thanks for the mobile," Stacie said. "It's darling, and it'll be perfect in the nursery."

Jenna smiled. "I couldn't resist it when I saw it. I knew you'd love it."

Stacie took a step back and considered Jenna. "You look great today, Jenna. Is something different?"

Nervously Jenna fluffed up her bangs. "Since yesterday? When would I have had time to do anything different?"

"I suppose not," Stacie conceded, "but something's different." She paused. "I saw you sitting with Dillon in church this morning. You looked a little chummier than usual."

Jenna smiled just a bit. "Well. . . ."

Jenna considered whether or not this was the right place to tell Stacie about last night and Dillon. Her answer came by way of an interruption.

"Stacie, dear," one of the older women said, taking her by the elbow, "I've heard a rumor that you are finally going to quit your job. I do think that's sensible, don't you, given the circumstances."

The moment had passed. All Jenna could do now was eavesdrop on Stacie's conversation.

"Well, yes, I am cutting back," Stacie said, "but I hope to work part time after a couple of months."

Donna joined the conversation. "Does this mean you finally found a replacement?"

Stacie nodded dramatically. "Finally. It's someone that Dillon knows. Her name is Sarah Martyn, and she's well qualified for the job. I have no reservations about leaving the shelter in her hands."

"Then why don't you just quit completely?" Donna asked.

Stacie was shaking her head now. "I don't think I could do

that. It's in my blood."

"But a baby is a lot of work and responsibility," the older woman commented.

"I know," Stacie answered, "and I realize it may be quite a while before I'll be ready to work full time again, but I know I'll stay at it. The Lord will work out the details, just like He has by bringing Sarah Martyn into the picture just when we needed her."

The conversation drifted away toward the seating area. Jenna inched forward in line but kept an eye on Stacie. How she admired Stacie. The copper-headed woman was one of the most tenacious people Jenna knew. She lived by the maxim that to obey God meant to find out what He wanted you to do, and then do it. And her convictions about what God wanted her to do were not tied just to the moment; she had a broader vision, a lifelong goal, a role she had carved out in a profession that meant something to her.

Jenna reached the head of the line and accepted a tray with cake, nuts, and punch on it. The seats around Stacie were occupied, but she easily found a place to sit a few feet away. She could not hear everything that was being said by the cluster around the rocking chair, but every few moments a phrase or laugh would lilt through the air to her ears. She hoped that it would not be long before she had a chance to confide in Stacie.

But what exactly would she say? Just that Dillon wanted her to stay at the camp? In the face of Stacie's certainty about what she should be doing, Jenna was newly uncertain about her own future. The euphoria of the previous evening and earlier in the day was wearing off. The reality was that Dillon had offered no commitment, nothing that would really tie her to St. Mary's or the Homestead. Obviously there was still a great deal they needed to talk about if they were going to be honest with each other about their feelings.

Jenna had come to a near-final decision to go to graduate school in the fall if she could get accepted with a late application. She had thought about it for hours at a time. It seemed like a sound decision. Graduate school would give her something tangible for the future, prepare her to devote herself to something she believed in the way Stacie did.

Had Dillon said or done anything that should change her mind? Could God's Will be changed by a simple kiss or by the warmth of a man's hand on her own?

Clearly she had a lot more thinking to do. She had given up expecting anything from Dillon and he had taken her completely by surprise. His kisses last night had been all the sweeter for their unexpectedness, and she had felt his face near hers for hours after he had gone. She reveled in the headiness of his affection, so long awaited. But why now? Why had he waited so long?

Jenna sighed as she bit into the sweet white cake with the raspberry filling. An hour ago she had hardly been able to keep her fingers off the cake. Now she was too distracted to taste it at all.

fifteen

When Monday morning came, Jenna was relieved that the day's agenda held nothing out of the ordinary. After the eventful and thought-provoking weekend, she was quite content to fix her thoughts on the mundane chores of looking after the camp grounds. Perhaps the answers she sought would come to her in the middle of the meadow or at the horses' trough or while straightening out the equipment shed. She looked forward to a day of predictability and sameness.

Jenna allowed herself to linger over a third cup of coffee and a doughnut, now growing stale, left over from Saturday. She pressed the warm mug against her cheek, remembering the coffee she had shared with Dillon Saturday night. It was just coffee; they had shared dozens of pots of coffee in the last two years. It was silly to feel sentimental about it. Yet she found herself choosing the mug he had used that night and holding it to her face, her eyes closed in thought.

Monday's list of chores would provide structure for her activities; she would do things she had done hundreds of times. But things were not the same, and Jenna knew it.

She had not seen Dillon since lunch time yesterday, when they had driven home from church together. She was not sure what to expect from him now. Would he go about his usual activities and invite her out formally? Would he join her when he saw her on her evening walk? Would he go out of his way to make their paths cross? This was a new beginning and she did not yet know what "normal" would be from now on.

Wondering about it made her jittery. Should she seek him out? Jenna did not want to assume too much about their relationship; neither did she want to assume too little. Just what had their encounter meant to Dillon? She hoped that they would soon have an opportunity to talk and establish a clearer footing for moving forward together.

Her coffee had grown cold and the last of the doughnut was too tough to be edible. She wrapped it in a paper napkin and tossed it in the trash on her way to the sink. Seeing that the dishes were once again creeping up on her, she hastily washed what had accumulated in the sink since Saturday night and set the assortment of dishes—mostly coffee mugs—in the dish drainer. It was time to get dressed and get down to work.

৵

Thirty minutes later she was outside, her hand poised to open the sports equipment shed. She knew for a fact that the last group to use it had simply shoved everything back inside and forced the door shut. Since then, getting ready for the workday had consumed all her time and she had not been near the shed. Now it was time to remedy the situation before the next set of weekend campers arrived.

Jenna pulled the shed's door toward her and instinctively crouched to catch the basketballs that tumbled out. Her hands and feet went in all directions in an attempt to block their escape. For the most part, she was successful, but one of them got away and she watched, dismayed, as it rolled down the slight incline of the front lawn and headed for the parking lot. It bumped to a stop in the gravel. She turned back to the shed. She would fetch the runaway later, after she had brought some order to the rest of the equipment.

The volleyball net was wadded up in one corner. Methodically she opened it up and wrapped it more neatly and tightly.

She moved on to standing six baseball bats upright and counting the softballs to make sure they were all accounted for. She picked up a frisbee off the floor and tossed it on an upper shelf. Jenna sighed and shook her head. She never understood why campers did not put things back on the shelves, but it was the same nearly every weekend. By Sunday night, every piece of equipment was part of one conglomerate heap on the floor of the shed.

"Missing something?"

Jenna looked up to see Dillon just outside the shed, balancing the runaway basketball on his fingertips. She smiled and reached out for the ball. "Thanks. I almost had things under control, but this one was determined to find freedom." She tossed the ball in the rubber trash can that already held assorted balls. "Whatcha up to today?" She kept her voice sounding normal and even and her hands busy.

"Oh, the usual. You know. There's still some cleaning up to do at the stable site."

"I'll be happy to help you with it."

He nodded. "Maybe after lunch." His eyes glistened as they caught the sun. He had something wrapped and tucked under one arm, and Jenna could not help being curious. Was it another gift? Was he finally going to reveal himself as the mysterious gift giver?

"Speaking of lunch," he said, holding the package out in front of him, "I've got some here."

"Lunch?" she questioned, squelching an impulse of disappointment. "It's only ten o'clock in the morning."

He shrugged. "Knowing you, you've already put in half a day's work. How about it?"

She raised her eyebrows briefly and then laughed. "Sure."

"We can walk up to the meadow," Dillon said. "By the

time we get there it will be ten-thirty, a more respectable time
to have lunch."

They took their time going over the hill, past the stable,
and around the curve in the road to the meadow. Her mind
automatically registered that the meadow should be mowed
before the weekend or the grass would be too high for softball.

"I don't get up this far as much as you do," Dillon said. "It
sure is pretty. Look at the way the light makes things shine."

Jenna nodded. "It's pretty bright out in the open, but over
there, under the trees, it's not so bad." She gestured toward a
fallen tree trunk on the perimeter of the meadow. "I like to sit
over there sometimes. It's out of the direct sunlight, but you
can still see the way the light plays off of everything."

"It's nice today," he said, taking her hand and leading the
way to the log. "Not so humid as yesterday."

"Mmmm. But that's only the start of summer. It'll get worse
before it gets better."

"Guess we should enjoy it while we can."

Jenna wondered when they were going to quit talking about
the weather and the sunlight and get down to why they were
having lunch together at ten o'clock in the morning.

Dillon unwrapped his bundle to reveal generous ham sandwiches and shiny red apples. A thermos held lemonade.

"It's not quite the spread you put out on Saturday," he said,
"but it'll stave off hunger."

"Looks great to me." Jenna reached for half a sandwich
and took a bite. "To tell the truth, I am kinda hungry, even if
it is early."

"I'll bet you're not a breakfast eater."

She smiled at his insight. "Not usually. Just on the weekends."

"So what do you think about when you sit up here?" Dillon asked.

Jenna gave a nervous laugh. "Oh, you know. Stuff. Life's big questions."

"Such as?" Apparently Dillon was simply not making conversation.

Jenna tilted her head thoughtfully. "Well, such as what to do with my life. I look at Stacie and really admire the way she knows what she wants and goes after it. She's passionate about her work, committed to having a family, and she'll do it all."

"I suppose a job cleaning out horse stalls is not something to feel passionate about."

Jenna was quick to correct a misconception. "I love it here, Dillon. Don't get me wrong about that. But I'm not sure it's the same thing. It's not a vision, a passion like I see in Stacie . . .or even you."

"Me?" He could say no more because his mouth was full.

"Yes, you. Look at the way you've thrown yourself into this camp. . .the financial risk you're taking, the dream you have for what it will be someday."

"But you have the same dream. I meant it when I told everyone on Saturday that I could not have done this without you."

Jenna looked away. "I know. But you were the one who got things rolling. I just jumped on board when it looked like it was going to work. It's your dream, Dillon." She was forcing herself to dissociate from the work that had been the bright light in her life for the last two years. As much as she loved the Homestead, she had to remind herself that it belonged to Dillon.

"And what's your dream?"

She shrugged. "That's part of what I come up here to think

about. For the last four years, I was just trying to get through college. Now I'm out and I don't know what to do next."

"I see," Dillon said softly. "I didn't realize. . . . I guess it makes sense that you would be thinking about a change. After all, you just graduated from college."

Puzzled, Jenna looked at his distracted profile. "When you asked me to stay for the summer, I thought. . . ."

Dillon was nodding. "I get it now. You thought I wanted you to leave when the summer was over." He set his half-eaten sandwich down. "I guess this is a prime example of the poor communication between the two of us."

Jenna was not sure what to say. She chewed slowly.

"So what are you thinking of doing?" he asked.

She waited a split second before answering, "Graduate school."

He looked at her, questions in his eyes.

She continued. "It's kind of late to be applying for the fall, so I might end up on a waiting list. I applied to three different universities. And if I can get in—"

"You'll go?"

Jenna did not answer, leaving Dillon to interpret her silence for himself.

"So you would be leaving the camp." His words were a statement, not a question. "And St. Mary's."

They were quiet for a few moments then. Dillon handed her an apple and she bit into it, the crunch sounding thunderous in the silence.

"You're smart," Dillon said, polishing the already shiny apple with his shirttail. "Graduate school is a good idea. It's a good way to build your future."

Her heart sank. She had hoped he would object to her leaving.

"Actually I had something I wanted to ask you," Dillon said, twirling the stem of his apple.

"Yes?"

"Well, now I'm not so sure about it."

"Oh, just spit it out." She took another bite of her apple, trying not to look as nervous as she felt.

"It's something I've been thinking about for quite a while, actually," he explained. "But lately, we haven't been talking as much as we used to and I wasn't sure I should bring it up."

"Bring what up?" She was getting quite curious now.

"A partnership."

She raised her eyebrows. "A partnership? What do you mean."

"Jenna, if you want to go to graduate school, that's great. I know you'd be an excellent student just like you were in college. And you'd probably get a good job in some lucrative business and have a secure future. But we've been working together for two years now, and I'm not sure I believe that that's what you want."

She did not know how to respond. What kind of partnership was he talking about—and why did he digress into the pros and cons of graduate school?

"Dillon, I'm afraid I'm not following you," she said.

"Let me back up. A partnership. I want to offer you a legal partnership in the Homestead. I think you love it here as much as I do and that you don't want to leave."

"Well, I. . .I. . .I do love it here, you're right. But a partnership? Wouldn't I have to buy into the camp? I don't have any money, Dillon. You know that."

He was nodding. "I realize that. There are a lot of details we'll have to work out, but I thought offering you a partnership was a way of letting you know how much I value the work you do around here. . .how much I value you and want to have you around."

"I don't know what to say." Such a possibility had never entered Jenna's mind. "I appreciate the gesture, Dillon, but I really don't see how it would even be possible. It would take—"

He cut off her protests with a wave of his hand. "I'm not giving up. I'll see my lawyer about it this week."

"Dillon, please—"

"It can't hurt to ask a simple question. A creative legal mind may come up with some asset that you don't even realize you have."

She was shaking her head.

"Just promise me one thing," he said, taking her hand. "Promise me you'll consider it if I can work out the legalities. Don't make a decision about graduate school until I can talk to a lawyer."

She sighed. "Okay. That's reasonable." She gave his hand a squeeze.

Dillon tossed his apple core aside, moved closer to Jenna, and took her in his arms.

sixteen

On the sixth ring Jenna finally got the door unlocked and flew across the kitchen to the phone. "Hello?"

"Me here."

"Oh, hi, Stacie," Jenna said gasping. "Just give me a chance to catch my breath."

"Were you outside?"

"Yeah." She took a deep breath and let it out. "Couldn't seem to get the door open. I think I'm okay now. What's up?"

"We didn't really get to talk on Sunday. I got the feeling that you wanted to, so I thought I'd call and check in with you."

Jenna took another deep breath. So much had happened in the last three days. Where should she begin?

"Let's just say your junior high shenanigans paid off."

"What!" Stacie screeched into the phone. "Did Dillon finally talk to you?"

"He did more than talk."

"Jenna! When did all this happen? Why didn't you call me?"

Jenna laughed at her friend's exuberance. "Everything's been so crazy the last few days. I'm still trying to sort it all out."

"Well, I want to hear everything. Oh. . .just a minute, Jenna. I've got a call on the other line."

Apparently Stacie was calling from the office, so they would have to keep this conversation short. As she listened for the click that meant Stacie had returned, Jenna rapidly inventoried everything that had happened between her and Dillon in the last couple of days. A telephone conversation prone to interruptions was not the way she wanted to handle this. She and Stacie needed time together, face to face.

"Back," came Stacie's pert voice. "Start at the beginning."

Jenna laughed. "I have a better idea. How about if I invite myself to supper tonight? We can kick Brad out of the room and have a good long talk."

"Sounds great to me. What time will you come?"

"Five o'clock? Will you be home by then?"

"I'll make a point to be."

"See you then."

Jenna hung up the phone with satisfaction. Dillon's midmorning lunch would tide her over for the rest of the day. Jenna was free to finish up her work within a couple of hours and head into town for some shopping before going to Stacie's to eat.

With a light step, Jenna left the cottage and went up the hill again, heading toward the stable. The day was growing quite warm; she wanted to be sure the horses had enough water before she left. Then she had a few phone calls to make to finalize arrangements for the group coming the next weekend. After that she would be free.

As she approached the stable, she saw Dillon hard at work stacking unused lumber off to one side of the project. With a stab of guilt she remembered that she had offered to help him with this task. She could see he was already sweating in the sun. Just then, as he paused to wipe his forehead with a handkerchief, he looked up and saw her at the crest of the hill. He smiled broadly and waved. She returned his wave and continued toward him, the thought of shopping gone from her mind. She would rather be stacking lumber with Dillon.

"Why didn't you holler for me?" she asked when she got within earshot. "I said I'd help."

"Thanks, but I don't think I'm going to finish now anyway. I've got a list of errands a mile long and I'd better get started on them." He paused for a second and his lips turned up at the corners. "Want to have dinner with me tonight? I'll even cook."

For a split second Jenna considered canceling dinner with Stacie to accept Dillon's invitation. But she said, "I'd like to, but I made some plans already. Can I have a rain check?"

"Only if you redeem it tomorrow."

"You've got a deal."

Dillon brushed his gloved hands together and shook loose a spray of sawdust. "Well, I guess I'd better get going. See you later."

Jenna nodded, "Later."

She watched for a moment as he followed the road toward his cabin to where his pickup truck waited. His gait was relaxed, confident, long. For the first time in two years, Jenna did not feel self-conscious about watching the way Dillon moved. At the bottom of the hill, he turned his head and smiled over his shoulder at her. The lump in her throat was one of fulfillment and satisfaction.

Jenna turned to her chores. She would just feed and water the horses and then be on her way. Shortly after she finished filling the water trough for the horses, she heard Dillon's engine approaching and turned to wave as he drove by. She had long ago memorized the distinct rattle of his used pickup. He rambled down the dirt road and the sound of the engine faded away. She was left with the quiet of the camp on a peaceful afternoon. Mandy, her favorite horse, nuzzled her face, looking for attention.

Jenna patted the animal's head. "Ah, Mandy, life is so simple for you. I'll bring you an apple the next time I come, promise." Jenna hoisted herself up on the fence and sat, contentedly stroking Mandy's neck. This was the first opportunity she'd had to take a closer look at the new structure. The size of the frame told her the new stable would be nearly twice the size of the old one and have a higher, bigger loft. She squinted her eyes and tried to visualize completed walls and neat, clean stalls. Part of her would be sorry to see the old building torn down, but she would be glad to have the new one finished.

Suddenly she gasped and flailed at the fence as something pulled her backwards. A strong hand gripped her face, keeping her from screaming. She kicked and thrashed to no avail. In only a matter of seconds her eyes were covered with a heavy blindfold and her arms were tied at the wrists behind her. She had been completely overpowered. Something hit her head with a thud. The last sound she heard was Mandy, braying her objections.

&

When she came to, she had an enormous headache. Her hands were still tied behind her; her shoulders had grown stiff from their awkward position. She tried to open her eyes, but the blindfold was tied even more tightly than before. Lying on her stomach, Jenna's right cheek was pressed against a cold, hard, gritty surface.

With a groan, she turned over and dragged herself to an upright position, glad to get her face off the dirty floor. She felt groggy, as if she had been unconscious for hours but, tied up the way she was, she could not see her watch. She tried to moisten her lips then spat out the dirt that had accumulated on her tongue. She instinctively strained at the scratchy rope around her wrists, but the only result was to scrape her skin.

As her mind cleared, she tried to remember exactly what had happened; the police would want to know later. Jenna did not allow herself to consider the possibility that there would be no "later" for her.

For two years she had walked the camp freely at any hour of the day or night, feeling completely safe. As she sat on the hard cold floor, stiff and achy, her mind filled with images of her evening strolls—the friendly shadows of the trees along the side of the camp's dirt road; the sounds of squirrels and raccoons rustling in the bushes, waiting for her to pass before they ventured out; the glorious spray of stars when she reached the open meadow and lifted her face to the jeweled night sky. Never had she felt any sense of danger, only luxury at living in such a setting.

When suspicious friends had warned her that she ought to be more careful, Jenna had considered them patronizing and paranoid. And now, something had happened, but not at night, not when the shadows could turn from friend to foe. It had happened in broad daylight, the middle of the day. But it might as well have been the middle of the night. Dillon had gone on his errands; no one else was at the camp.

Desperately Jenna wanted to know what time it was. Had she been missing long enough for anyone to notice? She thought of Dillon returning from his errands to find her gone— but she had told him that she had plans, so he would not expect her to be home. Stacie—Stacie would be the first to miss her. Jenna bent her face down against one shoulder and tried to wriggle the blindfold out of position. She worked at it as hard as she could, but eventually let her shoulders sag in resignation. The blindfold would not budge, and she was just making her shoulder more sore.

My feet are loose, she suddenly realized. Tentatively she started scooting around the floor, with her feet out in front of her as antennae. She moved in several directions without hitting any objects. The room seemed to be empty. But where was a door or a window? *Where am I?*

With great effort she pulled herself to her feet and began taking tiny steps forward. The last thing she wanted to do was bump into something, hurt herself, and spoil any chance she had of getting out of wherever she was. Tediously, probing every step with one foot, she inched forward. It was hard for her to judge distance or time under the circumstances, but she kept at it till she was sure she had gone at least ten feet. Apparently it was a big room. She wondered if she had chosen the wrong direction. Had she been only two feet away from a door in the other direction?

Finally her toe hit the wall and she was flooded with relief at this small triumph. Arbitrarily she chose to keep moving to the right and follow the line of the wall. She had not yet bumped into any furniture and had just about concluded that the room was empty—dirty, big, and empty. Where was she?

She hugged the wall and kept moving, going a little faster as she became more sure that she would encounter nothing in her way. She kept one shoulder pressed against the wall, feeling for a window; one foot dragged along the baseboard looking for a door.

Suddenly she heard the crunch of footsteps outside the building. Desperately she cried out, "Help! Help! Someone help me!" At the thought that someone might come to her aid, she at last gave in to the impulse to sob.

The door opened. She turned toward the sound, realizing that she had not been far from finding the door.

"Nobody can hear you," said a man's voice.

I know that voice, Jenna thought. Aloud she said, "Who are you?"

"Well, now, that's a good question. If you had paid any attention to me, you'd know who I was. And you wouldn't be in this predicament."

Jenna's heart sank. She did know that voice. *Doug.* She felt foolish for thinking help had come. Instead, things were going to get worse.

Her heart pounded. "Doug, whatever the problem is, let's talk about it. Is all this really necessary?"

"You brought it on yourself."

Rage welled up inside Jenna—what a ridiculous notion! But her fear and instinct kept her in control. "Why don't you untie me and we'll talk?"

"You really do think I'm stupid, don't you?"

Jenna backed off immediately, "No, of course not, Doug. You're not stupid." The voice inside her head told her that she had to keep him happy or things would get worse, much worse. "I consider you a friend, so I'm surprised at all this."

"Hah! A friend!" he scoffed. "I made one little mistake and you cut me off. Some friendship."

"Please, Doug, at least take off the blindfold so we can talk face to face."

She felt his tall form come nearer and forced herself to stand perfectly still. With surprising gentleness he reached around to the back of her head and untied the knot. The cloth fell to the floor.

"Thank you, Doug. That's much better." Jenna had to call up every ounce of courage to keep calm, and so far she was succeeding. She quickly glanced around the room to get her bearings and looked out the window. It was dusk. She had been there for hours, lying unconscious on the floor.

The room was bare and covered with layers of dust. Jenna recognized it as a remote cabin that she and Dillon had not used since taking over the camp. There was a lone bunk in the room, though it could easily have held beds for ten people.

In only a fraction of a second, Jenna's attention was fixed again on Doug. She saw now that he had brought food on a tray from the camp dining hall. Her fear and anger had obliterated any appetite she might have had at this time of day. But she knew she should eat—both to keep up her strength and to keep Doug happy.

"Sorry that the place is so bare," Doug said, setting the tray down on the floor. "I wanted to get you a table. . . ."

But all the other cabins were locked. Jenna supplied the rest of the sentence in her own mind.

She looked at the food and tried to brighten up. "That looks good. Are you having some?"

He shook his head slowly and gestured that she should sit and eat.

"My hands," she reminded him.

He stepped behind her and untied her wrists. She resisted the urge to rub them and she simply sat down on the floor, next to the tray. The plate held a slice of ham and some vegetables, and there was a glass of milk. Jenna picked up the fork and forced herself to break off a piece of ham and put it in her mouth. Doug had made some attempt to heat the food, but it had, of course, grown cold. She ate in silence, with an occasional glance at Doug. Every bite seemed to lodge in her throat. She used the milk to force the food down.

Doug began twirling a piece of rope in his fingers. Then he stuffed it in his pocket and pulled out a chain and a small lock. Horrified, she realized that he meant to chain her up and leave her all night. Her heart pounded so loudly she could not hear herself think.

"The bed," he said gruffly when she had finished her food.

"Doug, please, be reasonable," she pleaded.

"Sure, just like you were reasonable. Move over there."

Her fright intensified, she complied.

"You can reach the bathroom from here," he said evenly, as if he were commenting on the fine weather. He chained her right ankle to the metal bed frame. "I'll be back in the morning with breakfast."

He left.

seventeen

Jenna dug the heels of her hands into her eye sockets to keep from sobbing. Fury pulsed through her body, tempered only by the uncertainty of what Doug might do if she lashed out at him, unrestrained. When she had first come to consciousness, she had not known who her assailant was. But she took small comfort in knowing his identity now; his motives and intentions were still a mystery.

The situation was so unreal, so incredible, something she would expect to see on a television movie. Chained to a bedpost! Frightened as she was, she refused to lose control and cry. She did not know why Doug was doing this, but she would fight him every inch of the way.

She tugged at the chain angrily, accomplishing nothing but making the metal dig into her ankle. Of all the days not to wear any socks. It was a relatively lightweight chain, probably something he used to hold down a light load in the delivery truck, with a makeshift cuff and lock on each end. Her fright intensified as she realized he had made this contraption himself, probably with her in mind.

Jenna stood up and experimented. She could move in a radius of about ten feet—a length carefully calculated to keep her from reaching the door or being visible through a window. Doug had left her within reach of the bathroom, so she figured she might as well take advantage of it. Maybe some cold water on her face would help her think more clearly.

As she reached the sink, she felt the tug of the chain; that

was as far as she could go. She used only her thumb and
forefinger to touch the gritty faucet, which had not been used
in years. It groaned at her intrusion. Awakened from their
indefinite slumber, the pipes inside the wall rattled violently.
But she did get water, brownish at first, then gradually clearing as it ran for several minutes. She knew from the sight of it
that she would not want to drink it, but it was probably all
right to splash on her face.

The whole bathroom was coated with grit and scum. Jenna
grimaced involuntarily at the filth. She had known this cabin
was up here, but it had never occurred to her to give it any
attention. She certainly never thought she would be spending
a night in it. She had a vague recollection of Brad's saying
that he did not think it was structurally safe.

Jenna leaned over the sink, threw some water on her face,
and stood up again. As she waved her hands in the air to get
them dry, she surveyed the cabin. She could not get to the
door or any of the windows while tethered to the bed, and the
bed frame, she knew from experience in other cabins, was
solid and heavy. The mattress was bare; there were no loose
objects lying around within reach. Doug had chosen his site
well; there was absolutely nothing for her to work with. She
might just as well be lying on the floor with her arms tied and
her eyes covered.

Once again Jenna stifled the cry burgeoning in her throat.
If Doug came back, she did not want him to find her crumpled
in the corner, her willpower broken and her resistance dissi-
pated. She would keep thinking and stay alert!

Sitting stiffly on the edge of the bed, Jenna rubbed her sore
wrists. She glanced at her watch, only to discover that the
crystal had cracked and the hands had stopped at one-thirty-
eight. That was when she had been sitting on the fence,

contentedly stroking Mandy's mane. She had no idea what time it was now. If only Dillon had not changed his mind about stacking the lumber, she would have stayed with him and would not have been alone and vulnerable. Or if only she had left for town directly from the cottage, without sidetracking to check on the horses.

For weeks she had been agonizing about her future, feeling unable to take control of her emotions and decisions. And now, in a fraction of a moment, when her right to choose for herself was threatened, she knew what she wanted—and it was not graduate school. Some would call her foolish for not planning for the future but, at that moment in time, what she wanted most was to always feel the contentment that she had known living at the Homestead.

Jenna shifted her position so she could put her back against a wall. The silence, so long her friend, only deepened her fear.

Then she heard it—the telephone. From this far away, the outdoor bell sounded faint, but she was sure she heard it. It was past supper time; she had missed her appointment with Stacie. From the degree of darkness outside the window, she knew she was close to two hours late for dinner. Jenna had never broken her plans with Stacie before. There was no question in her mind that Stacie would scour the county for her.

Jenna had already realized that Stacie would be the first to miss her, but Stacie was nearly an hour away and would have no way of knowing where Jenna was. The phone rang insistently thirteen times before going silent. Jenna's heart sank as the last reverberations of the bell faded away. As long as the phone had been ringing, she had felt a link to Stacie, a lifeline to safety.

I'm here, Stacie, I'm here, Jenna's mind cried out. *Please, help me!*

Abruptly, Jenna sat up. What if Stacie did try to help? What if she tried to come out to the camp? Brad had made his feelings very clear: Stacie was not to come out to the Homestead alone while she was still pregnant. So far Stacie had been honoring Brad's wish, but she might set that aside to come look for Jenna.

"Just call someone, Stace," Jenna said aloud, her voice breaking hoarsely. "Don't try to come out here yourself."

She sank back against the wall again. Stacie was really her only hope, and she could not come herself. And even if she did come, Stacie would not think of hiking up to this remote building. She probably did not even know it was up here, tucked among trees and brush that had not been tended for years. Stacie would not think of this place—no one would.

The phone rang again, this time seventeen rings. Hope flickered in Jenna's heart. It had to be Stacie trying to reach her. No one else would wait that long for a phone to be answered. At least someone knew she was missing.

Jenna looked again at her stopped watch, then ran her fingers through her hair, brushing her bangs out of her face. Her hair was sticky and tangled and clung to her neck.

Why was Doug doing this? There had been other men whom Jenna had decided not to see. There had been one to whom she had nearly been engaged before she broke off the relationship. Doug was taking this all out of perspective. After all, they hardly knew each other. There was no relationship to break off. She would not have minded if Dillon had continued to buy his building supplies at the store Doug worked at. He could have continued his deliveries and the playful exchanges they had shared before their disastrous date.

Why? Why? What was Doug doing? What did he want from her?

Jenna's mind flashed back to the first time Doug had come to the camp with a load of lumber. It had been the previous fall, just as the weather was turning cooler. Dillon was trying to shore up one last set of cabins before suspending construction work for the winter. Dillon had been surprised to see Doug; he recognized him as someone who worked inside the store, not the one who drove the delivery truck. Doug had said he was just filling in for someone who was sick. But after that, he was always the one to bring Dillon's supplies.

It was odd, Jenna realized now, that Doug never seemed to have the full order with him. There was always some reason why not: they were waiting for a back order; the load was too big for the truck; he had overlooked a whole column on the order form; and half a dozen other reasons. Much too often he had a reason why he would have to come back the next day with the rest of the order. Doug had acted like this sort of thing happened all the time. Jenna had never paid much attention to it. Doug was bringing what Dillon needed; if Dillon was not bothered by the frequent incomplete orders, then why should it matter to Jenna?

When he had come for the first time, that day last fall, Jenna was sitting outside at the picnic table. It was really too cold to be sitting outside with her paperwork, but she had been stubbornly hanging on to the last vestige of warmth in the air. As the sun began its westward descent, its rays were blocked by trees, and the chilly fall air pricked her skin with none of the sun's comfort.

"Aren't you cold?" Doug had asked as he jumped down out of the cab of his truck.

Jenna had shivered and said, "No, it's a beautiful day." Then she had looked at him and smiled. "Are you new? Where's Max?" Max had been coming to the camp for over a year.

"Out sick. I'm filling in." He extended his hand. "My name's Doug."

She had returned his friendly gesture. "Jenna. Nice to meet you."

Doug had stretched his hands over his head and said, "Actually, I've been envious of Max's route. I like driving out in this part of the county."

"Most people think it's the boonies and wonder why anyone would want to come out here."

"Not me," he insisted. "This is great country."

Dillon had shown up about then. He seemed to recognize Doug from the lumberyard. The three of them had chatted longer than Jenna meant to until she finally had to admit that she was cold. When she was sure her sweater had rendered all the warmth it could provide, she had gathered up her papers.

"I'd better let you guys get back to your boards," she had said. "The light won't last long at this time of year."

She had let herself in the back door of the cottage. Doug had waved at her through the window before he and Dillon climbed in his truck and headed up the hill.

After that, Doug was the only one to make deliveries to the camp. Dillon reported that he still saw Max around the lumberyard, but they saw more of Doug. Jenna was beginning to put the pieces together now. Doug not only made twice as many trips as should have been necessary, but he also had acquired an uncanny sense of her activities. He consistently arrived when she was engaged in an outside chore. Most of their encounters had seemed casual and accidental. Now she was not so sure.

During the winter they saw less of Doug. Dillon involved himself with inside work, smaller projects, and plans for

promoting the camp in its new and improved state. But, as
Jenna reflected on it now, Doug had still managed to make
several trips out during the winter and to speak to her each
time. With the spring, construction work resumed, and Doug
was there twice a week. Several times she had offered him
something cold to drink; now she saw how he had used the
opportunities to linger and talk.

They never really talked about much. Perhaps that was why
Jenna had never taken Doug seriously. Though he would linger for forty minutes sometimes, the conversation never pro-
gressed beyond chitchat or social niceties. Doug was simply
someone who rippled the camp's midweek routine, at least in
Jenna's mind. Now she could see that he had a whole different viewpoint.

I've got to get him to talk to me, she thought. She realized
she did not know him well enough to predict how he might
think, so getting him to talk could be risky. On the other hand,
it could be her only salvation from this cabin prison. If she
could find out what it was that troubled him, perhaps she
could find some way to placate him long enough to get out.

For hours she sat on the bed, calculating what she might
say to Doug, how she might behave toward him. And she
prayed.

Jenna estimated the time to be about midnight when she
heard the phone ringing again. Her heart nearly stopped beating as she counted the rings. Stacie was not giving up. But
what about Dillon? If he had returned to the camp that afternoon, he would not have come up this way. Jenna remembered his earlier dinner invitation; clearly he had intended to
come back. Now the question was whether he would hear the
phone. For months she had teased him about his hermitlike
existence, with no phone in his cabin. He insisted he enjoyed

the quiet. So now she had to hope he would hear the phone and answer it before Stacie gave up.

She pulled her knees to her chest and wrapped her arms around them, ignoring the clattering of the chain. She propped her chin on one knee and listened, with her heart in her throat, for any change in the night sounds—footsteps, an engine, anything. But there was nothing. Hour after hour, there was nothing.

Eventually she reached for the tattered blanket Doug had left. Exhausted, Jenna gave in to sleep shortly before dawn.

eighteen

Jenna did not sleep long, for the light came soon. She had fallen asleep upright with her head awkwardly bent toward the wall. When the light wakened her and she tried to lift her head, pain shot down into her shoulder. She cried out against the pain, then opened her eyes and saw anew where she was.

The window across the room faced east. She knew from two years of mornings at the Homestead that the mornings were magical. Pink light danced on the leaves and left a sparkling trail through the bushes as the sun pushed its way upward into the sky. Jenna loved the mornings. In the summertime she often dressed early and took her coffee out to the picnic table and exhilarated in the daybreak splendor.

She could see none of that today. The window was small, the glass was smeared with the dirt of uncounted years, and she was trapped across the dingy room. The light penetrated enough to wake her, but she could take no comfort in the beauty she knew was just outside the cabin door.

Jenna pushed the blanket aside and got up and went into the bathroom. As scummy as it was, she was grateful it was there. At the sink, she braced herself for the splash of cold water on her skin. With one finger, she rubbed away the grime on a few square inches of the mirror and peered into it. A pale, sallow face with black blotches around the eyes stared back at her. Her hair had gone stringy overnight and badly needed combing.

At the moment, Jenna did not care how she looked. But in

the early hours of the morning it had crossed her mind that Doug might care how she looked. If she looked like she had made an effort to groom herself even under these conditions, perhaps he would be pleased and more inclined to talk. Then maybe she could apply the strategies she had devised during the night.

She wet down her hair the best that she could and used her fingernails to get the worst of the knots out. Cold water on her face seemed to help the blackness around her eyes. She straightened her collar and smoothed out her cotton slacks. This was the best she could do. Her appearance was still dismal, but it would have to do.

Jenna returned to the bed and waited. By this time she had been awake for a couple of hours. Doug had promised to bring breakfast; surely he would come soon.

At last she heard noises outside. For a fleeting instant, she hoped and prayed that it was anybody but Doug, but of course she knew it would be him. She swallowed hard and sat up straight on the edge of the bed.

He entered with another dining hall tray. This time he brought orange juice and cold cereal and milk.

"I hope you're hungry," he said as he set the tray on the bed beside her.

Jenna tried not to show any reaction to his incredible calmness. His tone of voice would have been appropriate in a restaurant or in a kitchen—or just about anywhere that she was not being held against her will. But here? How could he possibly act like this was normal?

Nevertheless, she took her cue from his tone. "Yes, I am. That looks delicious." She picked up a spoon and stirred the corn flakes. "Have you already eaten?"

"Yes, thanks." Being careful not to unbalance the tray, Doug sat down at the other end of the bed. He wore fresh clothing and had shaved. But his clean-cut appearance was deceiving, and Jenna did not like him so close. She moved the tray to her lap and started eating. She choked on a mouthful of cereal but forced it down. Doug sat silently, watching her eat. Every bite was an effort. Mentally she prompted herself: hold the spoon steady; chew; swallow; drink some orange juice.

At last she was finished. "Thanks," she said, looking him in the eyes. She hoped she appeared amiable but she also desperately searched for any indication of his frame of mind.

"I thought maybe we could talk today," she said quietly, tentatively.

His tone was smooth, but his words pierced her. "I'm sorry I had to go to such lengths to get your attention," he said.

"I'm sorry, too." She was not sure if she should say any more or hope that he would start talking.

"I never wanted to hurt you, Jenna. I love you."

"I've enjoyed our friendship, too, Doug," she said, choosing her words carefully.

Doug got up and shuffled across the room. "But that's all it is to you, just a friendship. You have a hundred friendships. Didn't you hear what I said? I love you."

Jenna sat perfectly still, hoping he would continue and open the window to his emotional state a little wider.

"You think I ran out of gas on purpose," he said defensively. "But that's not true."

"I'm sure you thought you had enough to get to the next station."

"Ever since that first day I met you, at the picnic table, I've known that you were special. And I finally got up my courage to ask you out. And you dumped me over something as stupid as gasoline."

"Oh, Doug, I'm sorry that I lost my patience that night. I should have apologized before now. But it wasn't really the gasoline."

"No?"

"I tried to explain before. The problem is me. I just didn't think. . . well, I'm just not ready. . . ." Suddenly, nothing she could think of seemed like it would satisfy Doug.

"You never even thanked me for the gifts."

Her ears perked up and she felt the color drain from her face. "Gifts?" she said faintly.

"Yes. The carved owl. . .the roses. I went to a lot of trouble for those things. I would think you could at least say thank you."

"I. . .I. . . ." Jenna fumbled for words. "There were no cards. I didn't know—"

"I suppose you thought it was Dillon."

His tone had turned decidedly sarcastic. Jenna's heart pounded.

"I honestly did not know what to think. As I said, there were no cards. But the owl is exquisite. And I loved the roses."

He scoffed at her. "It's a bit late for that, don't you think?"

Jenna swallowed hard. Rather than calming him down, she had riled him. Perhaps it was better to say nothing.

"It's written all over your face how you feel about him, you know. Anybody can see it. If he weren't such an idiot, he'd see it for himself."

"Dillon and I are good friends," she offered feebly. She dared not tell Doug the truth about her relationship with Dillon right now.

"What do you see in him?"

"I thought you liked Dillon," she countered. "You always acted like you enjoyed being around him."

Doug shrugged. "He's okay, I guess. But he thinks this camp is the only thing in the world that matters."

"He's dedicated. It's a wonderful thing he's doing."

"Well, he's still an idiot. And I don't know why you would defend him, considering the way he treats you."

Now Jenna was getting riled. "I don't think you should talk about him that way." Instantly, she regretted her words.

Doug sneered. "You can forget about Dillon Graves. He's not interested in you. I am. So let's move on from here."

Move on? her mind questioned. *Move on where?* She watched wordlessly as he opened the door and leaned out to pick something up. He set a cooler on the floor in front of her.

"I have some things I have to do, so I'm not sure when I'll be back. I made you some sandwiches, and there's some pop in there. Diet, of course. I know you like that."

"Thank you," Jenna managed to croak. The air had gone out of her fiesty resolve with his last sneering insult of Dillon.

"I should be back for supper." Once again his tone had transformed. Gone was the caustic edge. "We'll talk some more then." Doug sighed. "I love you, Jenna. I don't want to hurt you. But I can't stand by and let you get mixed up with someone like Dillon Graves. You don't deserve that."

And I do deserve this? she screamed mentally.

"I just want to take care of you so we can be together." He looked at his watch. "I'm already late for work." He stepped nearer and stroked her hair. His hand moved down to her collar and came to a rest on her shoulder. "I'll bring you some fresh clothes. I'm sorry I didn't think of that this morning. Is there something special you would like?"

The thought of Doug prowling around the cottage, going through her clothes, made Jenna shiver involuntarily. She answered simply, "No."

Doug picked up the blanket and wrapped it around her shoulders. "This cabin doesn't get enough sun to be very warm, does it? I'll be sure to bring another blanket."

His hand grazed her cheek tenderly. She stifled her repulsion and resisted the urge to cringe away from his touch.

Bending over close enough to her that she could feel his breath, he picked up her breakfast tray. "I'll try to be back early."

As soon as he was gone, Jenna threw off the blanket and jumped away from the bed. She paced back and forth as much as her leash allowed, gasping for air and groping for control over her emotions. "Oh, Lord, deliver me!" she cried out. "Tell Stacie what to do!"

nineteen

The hours of the morning crept by. For long stretches of time, Jenna thrashed against the chain and paced briskly back and forth as much as it would allow her. When she could no longer tolerate the irritation of the cuff digging into her bare ankle, she sat on the bed and massaged her tender foot.

The one thing she refused to do was cry—she would not give Doug that satisfaction.

Jenna's fear had now been consumed by her growing anger. In her rational moments she knew that she had good reason to be afraid of Doug. Clearly he was unbalanced, and she had no way to predict his behavior or to know what might anger or soothe him. On the other hand, Doug had already gone too far with this crazy plan of his; she would not sit by and let him go further without protesting.

She pictured him in his jeans and a tee shirt, what he usually wore when he made deliveries. Why had he given up a job inside the store to spend all day driving around the county in a rickety old truck with no shocks? Was it just so he could see her occasionally? Their first meeting had probably been truly accidental; he had simply been filling in for a sick driver. But after that—why hadn't she and Dillon questioned the change more closely when it had happened? At the time, it had seemed reasonable enough that Doug's and Max's assignments had been changed. There could be a hundred different reasons for the trade.

And one of those reasons could be because Doug asked for

the change. It seemed more and more clear to her now.

The carved owl. She remembered now that Doug had been working in the background on the day that she had first showed her budding collection to Dillon. A UPS truck had arrived with a package, a porcelain owl she had ordered from a specialty catalog. She and Dillon had sat at the picnic table chatting about her new hobby. At the time, Jenna had not paid any attention to Doug. He had seemed to be working steadily. Now, as she pictured the scene in her mind over and over again, she saw that he had been within hearing distance; he had been close enough to see what she had held in her hand.

And the roses. Dillon could not possibly have left them and, if she'd had her head on straight last Saturday night, she would have realized that. The Homestead was too far out of town. No one around the camp sold roses or any other kind of flower, especially late at night. Dillon would not have had time to drive into town and back again. Doug, on the other hand, had left a long time before Dillon. Doug had had plenty of time to go and come back. The roses had been his attempt to change her mind after she had said she did not want to see him again.

Jenna slapped herself on the head. *How could I have been so stupid? When will I learn not to think with my emotions?*

She pictured the roses displayed in a glass vase on the oblong wooden table in her cozy dining room. They were still there. *The first thing I'll do when I get out of here is throw those things away! And I will get out of here!*

Jenna turned toward the eastern window of the cabin. The light did not seem as bright as before, so she calculated that it must be early afternoon. Frustrated, she sat down hard on the bed. With one finger, she flipped the lid of the cooler and inspected its contents. Two thin ham sandwiches, a brown banana, and two cans of pop. Although she hated to admit it, she was hungry, and she did not want to succumb to the weakness that not eating would bring. She needed a clear mind.

With a grimace, she unwrapped one of the sandwiches and bit into it. At least this time Doug was not standing there watching her eat, so it was a little easier. She started to peel the overripe banana but immediately decided that it was too squishy to handle. She dropped it back into the cooler. She would save the other sandwich for later, in case Doug did not come back.

Abruptly, she stood up. "This is crazy," she said aloud. "I'm rationing food in case he leaves me here. I will not stay here!"

She whipped around and examined the bed. Maybe there was something she could unscrew. Gripping one side of the mattress, she heaved it off the frame and onto the floor. Next came the grid of springs that simply sat on the metal frame. It was more bulky than heavy. She wrapped her fingers around the coils in the middle of the springs and grunted. A moment later, she set it down on top of the mattress.

Now Jenna could get a good grip on the bed frame. She knew it was heavy, but she could be stubborn. With enormous determination, her teeth clamped together, she dragged it away from the wall. The metal legs scraped on the cement floor of the cabin. She ignored the shivers the sound sent up her spine. Now she could look at the frame from every angle. She stepped into the opening and, with her fingers, felt along the inside edges for screws. There was one place where the frame had been welded together, but surely it was not all one piece. She gave an exuberant shout when she found a screw holding a brace under the front legs.

Jenna spread her fingers out in front of her and studied her fingernails. Because of the amount of manual labor she did, she kept them fairly short. But they were all she had to work with. The screw, however, had been untouched for years and was so thick with dirt and rust that she could hardly find the groove. She scraped away at the black, sticky substance and slid the nail on her right thumb into the screw. Jenna tried to rotate her hand, but the screw would not move. She tried once more; the nail split.

"Ow!" she cried, jerking her injured thumb into her mouth.

She heard sounds outside and the door opened. Jenna panicked as her eyes darted around the room at the mess she had made, evidence of her intentions.

"I guess you don't like the bed," Doug said, his steely eyes fixed on Jenna.

She did not answer, just stared back at him.

"Let me just get that out of your way, then." Doug grabbed the end of the mattress and dragged it out the door. He came back a moment later for the springs. When he returned, he closed the door solidly behind him.

Fear raced anew through Jenna.

Doug crossed the room and glanced in the cooler. "I see you ate something. That's good."

Jenna was too angry to attempt conversation. "I want you to let me out of here," she said hoarsely.

"I can see that," he answered. "But I'm sorry. I can't oblige you."

"Why not?"

"I need you, Jenna. I want you. If this is the only way I can have you, then I'll take it." He gestured around the room. "Of course, we can't stay here. We can move away, though. You were thinking about leaving anyway, weren't you?"

How did he know so much about her, she wondered.

"We could find some place where you could work on your MBA."

She stared at him, unbelieving. Did he really think she would move away with him and live a normal life without trying to leave?

He checked his watch. "I can't stay long. I just came to see if you needed something. I haven't had a chance to get you any clothes yet."

"Don't bother."

Doug reached into his jacket pocket. "I'm not sure I'm comfortable with this arrangement." He pulled out the rope and blindfold. "I think the first way was better."

Jenna jumped up and tried to back away from him, waving her arms so he could not get hold of her. The resistance from the chain nearly threw her off balance. It was no use. He was too strong, too big for her to resist. He tied her wrists behind her and gave the rope an extra tug.

"I know how you like the sunset," he said, "so I won't cover your eyes. But you never know when someone might pass by here. We wouldn't want them to know you're here."

With one swift motion, he swung the cloth around in front of her and pulled it across her mouth. Using one finger, he forced it between her teeth, gagging her.

"I'll be back. Then we'll figure out what we're going to do."

And he was gone again.

Jenna screamed into the gag. She sank down against the wall to the floor, her shoulders shuddering from both fright and rage.

I blew it, she told herself. *I should have stuck to the plan to talk my way out of here. Making him angry is not going to help.*

There was no point in trying to move around. She leaned

her head back against the wall, hoping to soothe the enormous headache that had erupted the moment Doug had left.

Gradually she gave in to sleep and slumped down.

ೲ

She woke abruptly and blinked her eyes rapidly as she tried to get her bearings. *The cabin. The bed. Doug.*

What had made her wake up?

She listened carefully. Yes, she heard something—an engine—and then a familiar rattle. *Dillon!* She was positive that was Dillon's truck rattling past.

Her cries were muffled by the gag, but she persisted.

The engine stopped. Her heart raced. It was no coincidence that Dillon was in this remote part of the camp. He must be looking for her.

Awkwardly she worked her way to her feet and stretched toward the roadside window. If only she could make him see her. But she was too far from the window. He would never see her unless he got closer. She jumped up and down, hoping that her shadowy motion would catch his eye and make him look closer.

Dillon! Dillon! I'm here!

Then she heard voices, two voices. She stopped jumping and stood perfectly still to listen intently. The conversation outside was low-key and muffled by the walls of the cabin, but she was sure there were two distinct voices.

Dillon, be careful. Please, Lord, don't let him hurt Dillon.

The pitch of the voices elevated. They were arguing. She could hear a little more now.

"Jenna. . .missing. . .not seen her. . .why would I. . .?"

Their voices rose more. Jenna could hear clearly.

"I told you, I haven't seen her."

"What are you doing up here, then?" Dillon challenged

Doug's denial.

"Just wanted to take a walk."

"You should have checked with me. This is private property."

"Sorry. Next time I will."

"No one ever comes up here." Jenna could hear the growing suspicion in Dillon's voice. "This part of the camp has not been used in years. The road is one big pothole."

"Look, if it bugs you that much, I'll leave."

Jenna could hear, but she could not see what was going on. The voices stopped abruptly and she panicked. Had Doug turned on Dillon? Or had Dillon finally believed Doug and left? She had not heard him start his truck up again.

Her heart was beating so fast she was gasping for air and was afraid she would faint. *Hold on! Hold on!*

Something crashed against the door and she jumped. She heard grunts and the smack of a fist on flesh. The door rattled again. *Thud. Thud. Thud.* Someone was being thrown against the door repeatedly. But who?

Against all reason, she screamed into the gag again.

At last the door broke open. Dillon, his face bleeding, ran across the room and enfolded her in his arms.

For a moment, she was content just to be able to lay her head on his chest, to feel the presence of someone she trusted. Then she twisted her head around and tried to talk. Swiftly Dillon untied the gag.

She gasped for air. "Where is he?"

"Outside. Unconscious. But I don't know for how long."

Dillon moved behind her and worked on the knot at her wrists. Finally, it came free.

"What about the chain?" Jenna asked. "He has a key."

"And I have a pocket knife." Dillon extracted a thin silver

gadget from his pocket and set to work on the ankle cuff.

"Have you ever picked a lock before?"

"Not since college, but this can't be so tough. Try to hold still."

Nervously she looked toward the open door. What if Doug came to?

The lock snapped open.

"Run!" Dillon said, grabbing her hand and pulling.

She winced with every step, but she did run. He yanked open the truck's door and literally shoved her in ahead of himself. With a glance over his shoulder, Dillon started the engine. Doug was beginning to move around.

Knowing that the road would deadend soon, Dillon put the truck in reverse and backed up.

Jenna's eyes were fixed on Doug. "He's getting up!" she screamed.

"It's okay now, Jenna. You're safe."

They roared past Doug just as he got to his feet.

twenty

"Do you need to see a doctor? Did he hurt you?" Dillon asked.

Jenna shook her head as she rubbed her stiff neck. "I'm fine, I think, at least physically. Just some scrapes and sore muscles."

Once safely away from the camp, Dillon had stopped at the nearest pay phone and called the police. They did not know yet whether Doug had been picked up, but Jenna felt much safer with Dillon close by. Now they were on the main road, approaching St. Mary's.

"They want you to come down to the station to make a statement," Dillon said.

Jenna nodded. She had expected that. "I'd like to get cleaned up first."

Dillon shook his head. "I think they want to see you first, take photographs, that sort of thing."

Jenna sank down into her seat. "I suppose I have to."

Dillon reached over for her hand. At last the tears broke loose. Her shoulders shuddered uncontrollably as she let out all the emotion of the last thirty hours. Dillon eased the truck over to the side of the road and stopped. Jenna needed no further invitation to fall against him and cry. His arms tightened around her, and then one hand gently stroked her dirty, stringy hair.

"I'm so glad you're all right," he whispered into her ear. "I was frantic when I couldn't find you."

Jenna sat up, sniffled, and reached toward the dashboard

for a tissue. "I was afraid you wouldn't realize I was gone. I hadn't even told you where I was planning to go."

"I couldn't figure out why you left your car," he explained, "unless you had a date and someone picked you up. . .but I didn't think that was the case."

"I was supposed to see Stacie," Jenna said, wiping her eyes. "We were going to have dinner."

He nodded. "That's what I found out. I had a funny feeling that something was wrong, so I kept driving up to the cottage to see if you were back. Finally, around midnight, the phone rang, and I got to it."

"Stacie?"

"Yes."

"She was the only one who knew I was missing. But she can hardly walk these days, much less look for me. I kept praying that Brad would be home or she would find somebody to help her."

"I went over there in the middle of the night. We were up all night, racking our brains, trying to figure out where you might have gone." He stroked her cheek. "The police couldn't help. You hadn't been missing long enough, according to their rules."

"How did you ever think to look up in that corner of the camp?"

"I had looked everywhere else for you, over and over again. The last time I drove around the loop, I felt an irresistible urge to take the side road up there." He kissed her forehead. "The Lord was with me. I'm sure of it."

Jenna put her head back down against his chest. Dillon continued talking. "You know, when a road hasn't been used for a long time, it's pretty easy to see fresh tracks. It didn't take me long to figure it out then."

"But Doug? Where was he?"

"Lurking outside the cabin. I surprised him when I drove up. He was just standing around, not doing anything. He had no chance to make up a story." Dillon shook his head. "I still don't know where he was hiding his car. He was certainly being careful. He just made one slip. He was in the wrong spot at the right time."

"I hate to think of what would have happened if you hadn't been there when he slipped up."

"The important thing is that I was, by God's grace." He patted her shoulder. "Let's get you to the police station. The sooner we get there, the sooner we get out."

☙

An officer was waiting for them when they arrived at the station. Doug had been picked up a few miles from the camp, speeding along on a highway that led toward the state line. They had caught up with him just before he had crossed it. A forensics team had been dispatched to the cabin to look for physical evidence.

Jenna gave her statement. Her injuries, though superficial, were photographed, and then she was checked out thoroughly by a doctor, even though she insisted she was fine. At last they let her get cleaned up and into some fresh clothing, keeping her own slacks and shirt as evidence. She was offered some jeans that were four inches too big in the waist, a belt, and a man's flannel shirt. Gratefully she took what they had and did the best she could to look presentable.

When she emerged into the waiting room, Dillon grinned broadly.

"Give me a break," she said. "It's all they had."

He laughed aloud and shook his head energetically. "No, it's not that. I just called Stacie's house and got Brad on the phone." He grinned again.

Jenna gasped. "The baby?"

Dillon nodded vigorously. "Two hours ago."

"But it's early. Everything's okay?"

"Everything's great. They're both fine."

"What did she have?"

Dillon's eyes went blank. "I forgot to ask!"

"Take me to the hospital! Now!" She was already halfway out the door.

❂

"She's beautiful," Jenna cooed, gazing at the six-pound, ten-ounce little girl in Stacie's arms. "I've never seen anything so exquisite."

Stacie grinned up at her. "I think I wanted a girl all along. She's perfect."

Jenna, with Dillon's arm resting across her shoulders, looked on as Stacie brushed one finger across her daughter's cheek. The baby's slumber was undisturbed. Her tiny eyes were squeezed shut and her chest rose and fell delicately with her quick breaths.

"And what about that hair?" Dillon asked, admiring the swatch of bright red atop the baby's head.

On the other side of the bed, sitting next to Stacie, Brad laughed. "If the fact that she looks like her mommy means she's going to be like her, too—"

"You'll have your hands full," Dillon agreed.

Stacie reached up with her free arm and grabbed Jenna's hand. "You are such a sight for sore eyes. I can't believe you came straight over here after everything you've been through."

"I had to! I admit that I feel like I'm walking around in the twilight zone, but when Dillon told me she'd been born, I couldn't stay away." She reached out and touched the baby's soft hair. "Now, let's get down to business. What is this child's name?"

Brad and Stacie looked at each other. "We figured that out a long time ago," Stacie said. "Her name is Margaret Joanna Davis."

"For Margaret Barrows and your mother," Jenna said. "That's so sweet. Margaret would have loved it."

"What would Margaret have loved?" A new voice entered from the hall.

The four already in the room simultaneously turned their heads toward the door.

"Megan!" Stacie squealed. "How did you—" She turned to look toward Brad, who was grinning. "The baby was born only a few hours ago. How could you possibly have gotten here this fast all the way from Arizona?"

Megan leaned over the bed and gave Stacie a quick squeeze. "I was already on the way. The plan was for me to get here before the blessed event, but in your usual efficient way you did things ahead of schedule."

"Wait a minute," Stacie said. "Stand back. Something's different." She studied Megan's form, then her eyes widened. "You're having a baby!"

"That's right! In about five months."

"You rascal! You never said anything, all those times we talked on the phone."

"Keeping this a secret from you was the hardest thing I've ever done. My own husband didn't think I could do it. But it was worth it to see your reaction in person."

"Congratulations, Megan." Jenna stepped over and hugged Megan. "That's wonderful news."

"Jenna?" Megan said curiously as she assessed Jenna's appearance. "What happened to you?"

"That's a long story for another time," Dillon said. "This is such a great moment that I can't help making it better." He turned and faced Jenna squarely. "Jenna, remember that legal partnership I talked to you about?"

Jenna nodded, confused about why he would bring that up now.

"I figured out a way for you to be half-owner without coming up with a cent."

She looked at him, puzzled.

"All you have to do is marry me."

Before Jenna could answer, a cheer broke out in the small crowd. She could hardly believe what she was hearing.

"Say something, Jenna," prodded Stacie. "Don't let him weasel out of this."

"You bet I won't." Jenna turned on her most professional tone. "Mr. Graves, I would be most delighted to finalize the details of this agreement at your earliest convenience."

And she wrapped her arms around him and kissed him boldly.

A Letter To Our Readers

Dear Reader:

In order that we might better contribute to your reading enjoyment, we would appreciate your taking a few minutes to respond to the following questions. When completed, please return to the following:

Rebecca Germany, Editor
Heartsong Presents
P.O. Box 719
Uhrichsville, Ohio 44683

1. Did you enjoy reading *Between the Memory and the Moment*?
   ❏ Very much. I would like to see more books by this author!
   ❏ Moderately
   I would have enjoyed it more if _____

   _____

2. Are you a member of *Heartsong Presents*? Yes   No
   If no, where did you purchase this book? _____

   _____

3. What influenced your decision to purchase this book? (Check those that apply.)

❏ Cover	❏ Back cover copy
❏ Title	❏ Friends
❏ Publicity	❏ Other _____

4. On a scale from 1 (poor) to 10 (superior), please rate the following elements.

___Heroine   ___Plot

___Hero   ___Inspirational theme

___Setting   ___Secondary characters

5. What settings would you like to see covered in *Heartsong Presents* books?

_____

_____

6. What are some inspirational themes you would like to see treated in future books?_____

_____

_____

7. Would you be interested in reading other *Heartsong Presents* titles?   ❏ Yes   ❏ No

8. Please check your age range:
❏ Under 18   ❏ 18-24   ❏ 25-34
❏ 35-45   ❏ 46-55   ❏ Over 55

9. How many hours per week do you read? ————

Name _____

Occupation _____

Address _____

City _____ State _____ Zip _____

Susannah Hayden

❀❀❀❀❀❀❀❀❀❀❀❀❀❀❀❀❀❀❀❀❀❀❀❀❀❀❀❀❀❀

___*A Matter of Choice*—Stacie's new job promotion could mean the end of her future with Brad. . .or the start of a new and perhaps better life with Dillon. What life is Stacie to have? HP14

___*Between Love and Loyalty*—Megan Browning and her friends are working frantically to keep the old Homestead Youth Camp running. Then Megan discovers that the young architect who has captured her heart is planning on developing Homestead into condominiums. HP69

_*The Road Before Me*—Overwhelmed by self-doubt, Julie Covington searches for an answer. At her grandmother's childhood home in Maine she finds comfort and solace in the writings of a young girl, a girl who walked the same road as the one before Julie. HP77

___*Between the Memory and the Moment*—Jenna seems happy living and working at the camp owned by Dillon Graves. After all, she's hopelessly in love with the much-older Dillon, and he genuinely appreciates her work. Still, Jenna feels compelled to move on. But to what? HP113

___*Farther Along the Road*—Julie Covington wants to be accepted as a serious artist, and she wants to possess a love as vital as the one her grandmother had for her first love. When Larry Paxton displays interest in her paintings, Julie begins to feel hopeful that both needs can be fulfilled. HP117

...Hearts ♥ng....

..... Presents ....

Great Inspirational Romance at a Great Price!

Heartsᵥng Presents
Love Stories Are Rated G!

That's for godly, gratifying, and of course, great! If you love a thrilling love story, but don't appreciate the sordidness of popular paperback romances, **Heartsong Presents** is for you. In fact, **Heartsong Presents** is the *only inspirational romance book club*, the only one featuring love stories where Christian faith is the primary ingredient in a marriage relationship.

Sign up today to receive your first set of four, never before published Christian romances. Send no money now; you will receive a bill with the first shipment. You may cancel at any time without obligation, and if you aren't completely satisfied with any selection, you may return the books for an immediate refund!

Imagine. . .four new romances every month—two historical, two contemporary—with men and women like you who long to meet the one God has chosen as the love of their lives. . .all for the low price of $9.97 postpaid.

To join, simply complete the coupon below and mail to the address provided. **Heartsong Presents** romances are rated G for another reason: They'll arrive *Godspeed!*

YES! Sign me up for Heartsᵥng!

NEW MEMBERSHIPS WILL BE SHIPPED IMMEDIATELY!
Send no money now. We'll bill you only $9.97 post-paid with your first shipment of four books. Or for faster action, call toll free !-800-847-8270.

NAME _____

ADDRESS _____

CITY _____ STATE _____ ZIP _____

MAIL TO: HEARTSONG PRESENTS, P.O. Box 719, Uhrichsville, Ohio 44683

YES 1-95